THE LONG ROAD HOME

THE LONG ROAD HOME

BY

SHIRLEY WILLIAMS

EDITOR: JANET DAMON

Order this book online at www.trafford.com
or email orders@trafford.com

Most Trafford titles are also available at major online book retailers.

Note for Librarians: A cataloguing record for this book is available from Library
and Archives Canada at www.collectionscanada.ca/amicus/index-e.html

Printed in Victoria, BC, Canada.

ISBN: 978-1-4269-1432-4

*We at Trafford believe that it is the responsibility of us all, as both individuals
and corporations, to make choices that are environmentally and socially sound.
You, in turn, are supporting this responsible conduct each time you purchase a
Trafford book, or make use of our publishing services. To find out how you are
helping, please visit www.trafford.com/responsiblepublishing.html*

*Our mission is to efficiently provide the world's finest, most comprehensive
book publishing service, enabling every author to experience success.
To find out how to publish your book, your way, and have it available
worldwide, visit us online at www.trafford.com*

Trafford rev. 7/28/2009

 www.trafford.com

North America & international
toll-free: 1 888 232 4444 (USA & Canada)
phone: 250 383 6864 ♦ fax: 812 355 4082

ALSO BY SHIRLEY WILLIAMS

ZIPPER, THE MISCHIEVOUS KID

AND

DUST ON THE DISHES

CONTENTS

INTRODUCTION

This book is purely fiction, from the story plot to the characters and including the cities and towns mentioned in it.

RUNNING AWAY

The young boy leaned into the gusty April wind as the rain beat upon his bare back. He shivered from the cold, but kept plodding on. He had no choice. He had no place to go. He could not turn back home. That was forbidden. He could only go forward and hope for something good to happen for a change.

The sun had set and it was getting darker and colder by the minute. He looked frantically about, searching for something, anything that would help him keep warm. The bar ditch was deep on this long stretch of country road. Surely there is a piece of plastic or an old coat, or even a cardboard box would help right now.

He was shaking violently. He had to find some way to ward off the cold! He began to jog, hoping the speed and effort would generate some heat in his system. Why were there no cars traveling this road tonight?

He hadn't eaten anything for three days and his strength was almost gone. He gave up jogging and walked again, panting hard. Then he saw something up ahead that gave him hope. He hurried along until he could reach into the ditch and grab the big refrigerator carton. It was soaked, but still holding its shape.

Lightning flashed, and then a loud clap of thunder followed. He jumped across the ditch dragging the box behind him. He propped it against the barbed wire fence to give it some stability, then crawled inside and fell on his face, completely exhausted. He slept soundly in spite of the rain and the cold.

The bright morning sun warmed the cardboard box and the boy inside. Marlin was unaware of the blessing and slept on. Finally, about mid morning, his empty stomach began to growl, awaking him. For a moment he didn't know where he was, and then it all came flooding back into his mind.

The painful memories and the hunger pangs in his stomach drove him from the temporary security of the box. He took to the road again. Someone must live along this road somewhere!

Near the crest of the hill, he could see a house beside the road. His steps quickened. Surely they would have compassion on a kid and give him something to eat.

He knocked at the door and waited. He could hear a voice inside and saw a light streaming through a doorway. Still, there was no response. He knocked again, louder this time. He waited, tears welling up in his eyes. Then, finally, someone spoke to him from the other side of the door.

"What do you want?' A gruff voice asked.

"Please Sir, could you spare a bite to eat? I'm really hungry!"

"What are you doing way out here all alone, anyway? Where do you live?"

Marlin hesitated. How much should he tell this stranger about what had happened he wondered? He probably wouldn't believe it anyway.

"It is a hard story to tell, Marlin said quietly, especially on an empty stomach." The door opened a crack and a well seasoned face peeked out at him. After a minute or so, the door opened, welcoming Marlin inside.

As his eyes swept around the little room, Marlin knew immediately that this was the home of a very poor and humble person. The furnishings were few and rustic. Yet there was a warm spirit about it all.

The man shuffled around the table in the tiny room.

"Come on in and sit. I'll rustle you up some grub. I guess you won't be too particular about what you eat, will you?"

"No Sir! Not at all! I am so hungry I would eat most anything, and be thankful!"

"What's your name? I don't remember ever seeing you around here before." He reached into an ancient looking refrigerator and brought out some beans and a cold, hard biscuit. Placing them on the table, he reached for a fork and tossed it in front of the boy.

Marlin tried to refrain from 'grabbing and gobbling' as he answered the questions.

"Marlin Morris is my name. No, I don't live near here. I came from down south. I think it is south of here. I may be confused. I walked in the rain and through part of the night, so I don't know where I am, really. I'm from Buckley or south of there anyway.

"What in the world is a young kid like you doing this far from home, nearly naked, on a rainy night like last night?"

"Well, Sir. Ah, ah, what is your name, Sir?"

"My name is Weston Cox. Everybody calls me 'Cox,' but you haven't answered my question yet. What are you doing here?"

"Mr. Cox, Sir, I do appreciate the food and the chance to sit at your table and eat and talk. You've treated me well, but if you don't mind, I'd rather not bother you with my hard luck tale. Maybe you have some work I could do around here to repay you for your kindness. Is that possible?"

The man studied him quizzically for a moment, not knowing what to make of him and his strange behavior. Marlin squirmed under the piercing gaze.

"I'll tell you what, Marlin, he said. I have some fence that needs fixed. You could help me do that, if it would make you feel better, but first you need a shirt. So saying, he stepped over to the wall which served as a closet and took his extra shirt off the nail and held it out to the kid.

Marlin's eyes filled with tears as he reached for the shirt. This gift was too much for the man to give, yet if he refused it, he knew Mr. Cox would be deeply hurt.

The two stood speechless for a moment, looking deeply into one another's eyes. Something happened between them in that few seconds. An understanding developed. A friendship sprang to life. It was an instantaneous, miraculous, father-son relationship such as neither of them had ever known before.

WORKING TOGETHER

"Put the shirt on, Son", Cox said as he turned to leave the house. He was emotionally shaken by what had just taken place and embarrassed by it. He had never called anyone 'Son' before either. He didn't understand what had come over him.

He glanced back and noticed that Marlin was following him. He opened the door of an outhouse behind the house and rummaged through spades, hoes, and bars, until he found the tools he needed to fix fence. He handed some of them to Marlin to carry. He gathered up some wire and staples for the task and tossed them into the bed of an old rusty pickup parked nearby.

Marlin wondered if this was the only transportation the man had. It didn't look very reliable. They got into the cab and Cox turned the key in the ignition. The engine sprang to life instantly and sounded good! He smiled approvingly at Cox, who returned the smile.

They bounced slowly over the bumpy terrain until they came to a water gap, torn out by heavy rain the night before.

"Bring that wire and the fencing pliers," Cox said. "I'll get the diggers."

Cox began to dig a post hole and without a word, Marlin began to take the broken wires loose from the posts. Cox took note of the skillful way Marlin handled the pliers.

"You've done that kind of work before, haven't you?" He asked.

"Yeah, I've been doing it all my life," he answered

"That's not very long though, is it?" Cox asked with a grin.

Marlin didn't respond to that remark. He was on guard concerning anything about his past. He figured if he told even his age, he would only stir up more curiosity.

The gap was repaired in record time and they moved on up the fence, looking for other broken wires or posts and replacing them. It was an enjoyable morning for Cox, who spent almost all of his time alone. Soon it was lunch time, so they circled back to the little house beside the road.

As they unloaded the tools and put them away, Cox stopped and leaned against the pickup, studying Marlin. "Hey Kid, you were a lot of help out there. I'm glad you came along. Let's go find something to eat."

After a meal of canned beans and more biscuits, Marlin rose to his feet.

"Mr. Cox, Sir. I guess I should get going now. I thank you so much for the food." He began to remove the shirt.

"Now, hold on here! What's the hurry? Where're you headed, anyway? You ain't even told me your story yet. Keep that shirt on. I gave it to you. Just sit down now, and let's have a talk!"

Marlin slowly slid down and sat on the chair. His expression spoke of torment and fear. He did not want to talk about it, but he felt that he owed Cox some explanation.

"I really don't want to talk about it, Sir."

"I can tell that you don't, but it will make you feel better if you do. Trust me. You don't have to tell the whole story right now. We'll do this a little at a time. I'll ask you a question and if you can handle it, give me the answer. Okay?"

Marlin took a deep breath and quietly said, "Okay."

"Where is your mother?" Cox asked gently.

Marlin dropped his head to the table and began to cry great wracking sobs. He wiped the tears on his shirt sleeves and tried to regain control, but it was no use. He had held the tears for a long time but now the dam had burst.

Cox sat quietly and watched the suffering boy, not knowing what to say or do. When the sobbing had subsided he spoke again.

"What happened to her, Marlin?"

"She died. She got cancer and died just last week." He began to cry again.

"Where is she buried, Marlin?"

"She's buried In the Bucklin Cemetery, near the gate, next to her mother."

"Where is your father?"

"He's dead too. He died before I was born."

"Are there no other relatives?" Surely you have some grandparents or aunts or uncles."

"If I do have, I don't know where they are."

Marlin raised his tear streaked face and looked Cox in the eye.

"I have a step dad, but he hates me. He has always hated me and I don't know why. My mother had to protect me from him many times or he would have killed me. When she died, he told me to leave or he would kill me. I had to hide in the bushes to even see her buried. Then I ran away. That's why I am here. I had to try to find some place to live.

"How old are you, Marlin?"

"I'll be twelve next month. They could have put me in a foster home but I was afraid it would be like my step dad. I would rather find work and make it on my own, if I can. Guys have done it before. I know how to work, so I should be able to make it, don't you think?"

Cox stood up. He was a small man, not more than 5 '7" tall and about 145 lbs. In fact the two were nearly the same size except through the shoulders and at the waist line.

"Marlin, I don't have much to offer you. I wish I did have. Besides that, I ain't ever had any kids, never even been married. I am a loner, for the most part. I don't even have a dog because I don't have the money to feed the rascal. But I'll do what I can to find you some work and a place to live. I know most of the folks around here and they are good people."

"You've done enough, Mr. Cox. You don't have to...."

"Now, don't argue with me. You're just a kid and you need a little help. Let's go for a drive and look at the country side. Maybe we'll get an idea out there."

MEETING THE BLACKS

As they drove along the country road, Marlin felt as though he had known Cox all his life. They just seemed to "click." He hoped they would be able to find work for him nearby. He wanted to maintain the friendship that had begun. He had hardly had any close friends while growing up, and certainly no meaningful father figure in his entire life.

A Sheriff's car approached from the opposite direction and turned on his flashing lights, signaling them to stop. Marlin instantly became nervous.

"Please Mr. Cox. Don't let them take me back there. I don't want to be put in a foster home!"

"Don't worry, Marlin. Just let me handle this. Okay?"

The Sheriff walked up to the pickup window and spoke to Cox.

"Is that your boy you have there?" He asked.

"Why do you ask? Has there been trouble around here?"

"No, not really, at least that we're sure of. There is a young boy missing. His mother died last week and his step father is a sorry piece of work. He was cruel to both the boy and his mother. He threatened the boy and ordered him to leave. The word is he wouldn't even let the kid come to his own mother's funeral! People are concerned that he might have killed the youngster. I was just driving around checking it out.

Marlin was trembling with fright and fighting back tears. He didn't know what to expect.

The Sheriff leaned over and peered into the cab at Marlin. He knew instantly this was the kid.

"Sir, please step out of the vehicle and come over here for a minute."

7

The two men stepped away from the pickup so Marlin wouldn't hear the conversation.

"I can see that that is the Morris kid. I am not here to cause any trouble for him or for you. I just want to make sure he is all right. Are you going to take responsibility for him?"

"You know Sheriff, I wish I could. He is a good kid and I could use his help around my place, but things are real lean right now. I don't think I could even put proper food on the table for him, let alone send him to school and all. He is scared to death that you are going to take him and force him into a foster home. He has had enough of the wrong kind of fathers. Do you have any suggestions as to what we could do for him?"

"Let me see your driver's license. I'll write down your address and do some checking. I might find a way to help you both. I'll drive back over here and let you know."

They shook hands and the Sheriff drove away. Cox slid back into the pickup seat and started the engine. Marlin was visibly shaken by the encounter and anxious to know what had transpired.

"Its okay, Marlin, you heard what the Sheriff said. He was just making sure nothing had happened to you. He's a good man. I think he will try to help you in whatever way he can.

"He's not going to put me in a foster home, is he?"

"No, he just wants to be sure you're okay."

"Maybe I should just 'hit the road' again. I don't want to get you into any trouble, Cox."

"You needn't worry about me. I can take care of myself. I have an idea."

At the next corner, Cox turned east. Soon a big house loomed on the horizon. As they approached they could see that it was well maintained. The grass was cut and trimmed, the flower boxes were ready for spring flowers, and there was no junk machinery cluttering up the homestead. Cox guided the pickup into the drive way and stopped.

"Who lives here?" Marlin asked.

"Be patient. You'll see in a minute."

A curious, young face peeked out from behind the drapes on the window. Then a man came out and strode toward them. Cox got out

8

and walked to meet him. They greeted one another cordially with a handshake, and began to chat.

"My name is Weston Cox."

"Jim Black is my handle. Are you from these parts?"

"Yeah, I live over the hill and to the south, on the Nalor place. It's not much but its home to me. I live alone. I've never been married."

"I see. Who's the boy?"

"That is what I came over here about. This boy has had a tough time. His father died before he was born and his mother just passed away last week. His step dad is worthless and mean, according to the Sheriff. He wouldn't even allow the kid to go to his mother's funeral. Then he ordered him to leave under the threat of death. He hid in the bushes to see his mother buried, and then he left without even a shirt on his back. He walked in the rain storm last night until he nearly froze to death, and ended up at my door. He's polite and appreciative and knows how to work. I'd like to keep him but I don't have a bed for him or food to feed him. I thought you might know somebody that could help the kid out."

Mr. Black stroked his chin thoughtfully. He was a good man. He was well respected in the community, but he had had a rough time as well. His own son had died in a freak accident on the farm a few months ago. He had two girls, but he sure missed his son.

"Does he know about my boy?" he asked Cox.

"No. I didn't mention it. He doesn't even know why I stopped here. We were just out for a drive. I'm real concerned about him and he's scared to death they will put him in a foster home. He's heard about how they sometimes get treated in foster care."

"I'll tell you what. Bring him into the house and I'll have my wife fix some supper and we'll all get acquainted. I'm not promising you anything. I'm just thinking. Understand?"

"I understand and I thank you!" As Mr. Black returned to the house, Cox went to get Marlin.

"That guy is Jim Black. He has invited us to have supper with him and his family. Come on!"

Marlin didn't need a second invitation. The thought of a home cooked meal was exciting to him. He was on his feet in an instant, and the two walked side by side up the walk. The front door swung open for them and Mrs. Black welcomed them with a friendly smile.

The wonderful aromas coming from the kitchen were tantalizing to Marlin. It had been quite a while since he'd had a home cooked meal. His mother had been too ill to cook for months and he had been doing the best he could. Between his step-father yelling at him and his own worry over his mother, he had not enjoyed trying to learn to cook.

In a very short time, Mrs. Black was calling them to the table. He sat next to Cox on one side while the two girls sat on the other. Mr. and Mrs. Black sat at each end. Before they began, they bowed their heads and Mr. Black asked God's blessing on the meal.

Marlin waited for the food to be passed to him. Although he was ravenously hungry, he forced himself to be patient. The fried chicken, mashed potatoes, creamed gravy, asparagus and salad slowly came to him, one bowl at a time.

He became conscious of the eyes of Black family watching his every move, but his own eyes were on the food before him.

With his stomach full, he sat up straight, flashed Mrs. Black a wide smile and said, "That was a wonderful meal, Ma'am. I thank you from the bottom of my stomach, ah, I mean, heart!"

Everyone chuckled and began to excuse themselves from the table. The men went to the living room and became engrossed in farm talk while the girls and their mother began to clear the table. Marlin sat and watched, not knowing which group he would fit into.

He gathered up the remaining dishes and carried them to the kitchen sink.

"Oh, Marlin, you didn't need to do that," said Mrs. Black. "We'll get those!"

"I want to help," he replied quietly.

"Oh, I understand perfectly, but you're our guest tonight. Now let's go see what the guys are doing."

As they entered the room, Cox stood up saying, "It's getting late, Marlin. We'd better get going."

Mr. Black followed them out the door and they exchanged greetings again as Marlin and Cox departed. Neither of them spoke as the truck rumbled along the rough road and pulled into the yard at Cox's place.

Marlin was concerned about Cox and Cox was concerned about Marlin. Still, neither one felt free to express his thoughts to the other.

"Come on in, Kid. I'll find you something to sleep on, or I could drive another nail in the wall and hang you by the collar for the night." They exchanged smiles and entered the little house. Marlin knew there was neither couch nor extra bed. There was no living room and only a small kitchen, with a small table and two wooden, straight backed chairs. Another room served as Cox's bedroom. There was an open doorway between the two rooms so Marlin could see that the only bed was a small army cot. A wooden apple box sat beside it with a lamp and a few books and papers inside and on top of it.

Cox pulled a cardboard box from under the cot and removed a tattered army quilt.

"Maybe you can find enough floor space to put this for the night," he said as he handed it to Marlin.

"Thanks! That will work, Cox."

In a matter of minutes, both of them were asleep. They had had a full day, but rather than a restful night, each one slept fitfully. Cox was wrestling with the dilemma of what to do for Marlin and Marlin was searching his mind for an answer for himself. It was evident that Cox was financially unable to give him a home. He wished with all his heart that it could be worked out, because Cox seemed to be the father image he had longed for all his life.

Finally, in the wee hours of the morning, Marlin got up and quietly searched for a piece of paper and a pencil. In the moon light, streaming through the window, he scribbled a short note of thanks. He struggled with whether to leave the shirt or not. Finally, he decided to keep it since Cox had been so adamant about it. He took a deep breath and slipped quietly out the door and into the night.

ON THE ROAD AGAIN

Cox awakened at dawn to find the boy gone.

"Now why did he go and do a thing like that?" He asked himself aloud. He hurried out the door and looked up and down the road, hoping for, but not seeing any sign of him. He returned for his shoes and saw the note on the table. Deep despair and loneliness suddenly swept over him. He buried his face in his hands and let out a long, low moan.

"Oh, God have mercy! Why is it that my life is one continual journey of disappointment and misery?" But he didn't have time for self pity. He had to find Marlin.

Marlin walked fast, trying to cover as much ground as possible before daylight. Somehow he knew that Cox would be looking for him, but he refused to be a burden to the man he so respected.

He kept going north, never taking a side road in either direction. He knew that it was always a possibility to go in a circle if you didn't know the territory. And he didn't want to end up back home where his step-father might try to kill him. His life wasn't very promising, but he didn't want to die either. He still had hope.

The sun was throwing steaks of passion pink into the sky and outlining the puffy clouds on the horizon as he jogged along. His mother had taught him to appreciate God's handiwork in nature, so the beauty of the sunrise reminded him of her.

True to his word, Sheriff Baker stopped by the Social Services Department as soon as the doors opened and talked to a social worker about what could be done for Marlin. The information he received was disappointing. He immediately drove north to Mr. Cox's home, arriving just as he left the driveway. They exchanged information and then left in opposite directions to look for the boy.

Marlin could see a town in the distance and quickened his pace. He hoped it was a small town and not a big city. He watched the signs along the road hoping to get a feel for the kind of place it was. The traffic had picked up as he drew nearer town. Suddenly a car slowed beside him.

"Hey, Marlin, how are you doing?" Marlin was surprised to see that it was the Sheriff who had been looking for him the day before.

"I just came from Mr. Cox's place. I promised him I'd try to find a way to help you out, and then let him know. I was just keeping my word."

"Were you able to find a way, other than a foster home or orphanage?"

"I'm sorry to say that I wasn't. The Social Services would give Cox some money to help him provide for you, but the little shack he lives in wouldn't meet their specifications. He's out looking for you, Marlin. He really took a liking to you and is concerned about you."

"That makes me feel good, because I care about him, too. That's why I left. I didn't want to cause him any trouble. Tell him that for me when you see him again, will you?"

"If you will get in the car I'll give you a ride to wherever you are going. I'm not arresting you or anything like that."

Marlin hesitated a moment and then got into the car. They had reached the city limits and he was still looking for the name of the town and the population.

"Oh, it's called Allentown, 200,000 good people and a few old soreheads," he read aloud. "That's a big town. It's too big for me. I was hoping it was small."

"Are you hungry, Marlin? I am." The Sheriff didn't wait for an answer. He turned into a drive in fast food place. "Let's get ourselves a burger."

The two were soon enjoying a big hamburger with fries and a cold drink. Marlin enjoyed the meal tremendously and couldn't thank the Sheriff enough.

"Where shall I take you now, boy?"

"Could you take me to the other side of the town? I want to look for a farm job. I know a little about what to expect from country folks."

"I'll be glad to. I'm happy that you don't want to stay in this town. It has the reputation of being a tough town. They have a high crime rate with a lot of rapes and that sort of thing. Both BOYS' and girls have been the victims. You must be on guard, Marlin, where ever you go. There are a lot of predators out there."

They reached the north side of town and slowed to a stop on the shoulder of the road. As Marlin stepped out of the car, the Sheriff handed him a card, saying, "If you need help or anything, give me a call. I'll get to you as quick as I can."

"Thanks!" Marlin replied as he studied the card and pushed it into his pocket. "I'll do that."

He stood and watched until the car was out of sight. It felt so good to have his stomach full and to know there were men in the world that really cared about a lonely, homeless boy. He was encouraged to keep looking for something good to come along for him, like a job and a place to stay. He longed for a place where he could feel useful and appreciated.

Cox fired up the pickup truck and backed it into the road. He figured Marlin wouldn't go south, since that was the direction from which he had come, so he headed north. He took every side road, east and west, as he hurried along. Finally he reached the residence of the Blacks. He knocked on the door and was greeted by a smiling Mrs. Black. He explained his mission and her smile turned to a look of real concern.

She explained to him that she and her husband had discussed the possibility of taking Marlin into their home, but needed more time to think about it. She hadn't seen the boy, and was very sorry he had struck out on his own like that.

Cox left quickly to resume his search. In the afternoon the Sheriff met Cox again and relayed the information to him about the lad. They both agreed that they had done their best and that they would have to let him find his own way in the world.

KIDNAPPED

About two miles up the road, Marlin began to see some farm places on the horizon. He wanted to present himself in a proper way, so he practiced his introduction speech as he walked along.

"Good afternoon, Sir. My name is Marlin Morris. I'm looking for work. If you need a hand around the farm, I'll work for board and room. I'm not picky about what I eat and I'll sleep in the barn, if you like. I would appreciate it if you could find it in your heart to give me a chance to prove myself." He took the card out of his pocket. "You can call this Sheriff and check up on me, if you like."

Satisfied that he had a good little speech ready, he turned east, intending to go to the next farm on the road. Suddenly, a car skidded to a stop beside him, causing a swirl of dust to engulf him completely. Before he knew what was happening, two men grabbed him and threw him into the back seat of the car. The car sped off at a high rate of speed as the two sat on either side of the boy gripping his arms tightly, while a third man maneuvered the car around the bend without slowing down. The car rocked and skidded back and forth across the graveled road threatening to roll into the bar ditch. The men all began to laugh as though it was some big joke.

Marlin was frightened out of his mind! What were they doing? Why had they grabbed him? Where were they taking him? What did they want with him?

There was no way to escape, and he knew words would be useless. He sat stiffly against the seat and trembled. He began to search his mind for reasons one would be kidnapped. Sometimes it was for money. He had no family and no money. It used to be for a slave? Those days were gone long ago. For--then he remembered what the Sheriff had warned him about. He was more afraid than ever.

Finally the car slowed, and the man on his right began to taunt him. "Hey, kid, have you ever had anybody "do you?" Then he laughed maliciously. The man on his right joined in and they began to pinch and poke Marlin and to be very rude and crude in their language as well as their gestures.

"We got ourselves a virgin!" They laughed. "We're gonna have fun tonight!"

Marlin began to think about all that his mother had tried to teach him about God and faith and prayer. He wished now he had taken it more seriously. He needed help and God was the only one who could know about it and do anything to help him. He began to pray in his heart, asking the Lord to save him from this terrible situation.

A few miles farther up the road the car turned into an isolated driveway and drove down a trail of a road a few hundred feet and stopped next to a dilapidated house. It was overgrown with weeds and briars until it was almost hidden from view. They dragged Marlin out of the car and into the dark, dirty, rat infested house. It looked as though it had once been a lovely family home. It was roomy and there were remnants of colorful wallpaper still clinging to the cracked plaster walls.

They shoved Marlin into a room and shut the door, only to open it again and send the driver in to guard him.

The room had no furniture, but was littered with mice and rat droppings, dead bugs and some dirty rags. It had one window, which had a broken pane taped with duct tape. A filthy curtain dangled from a broken rod in front of it.

The guard dragged a wooden chair across the floor with a loud scraping sound and set it against the inside of door. He dropped his heavy frame onto it as though he was drunk, stoned, or extremely tired. Marlin couldn't tell which. He was just glad to be left alone.

The guard/driver ran his eyes up and down Marlin, as if looking for some stimulating aspect of his young slender anatomy. Marlin shivered at the thought of what the guy was planning. He looked out the window, studying the landscape, hoping to have an opportunity to escape. He had to have a plan.

16

The seconds dragged by. It seemed to Marlin that he had been trapped here for hours, when it had actually been only a few minutes. The other two men were making a lot of noise outside the door. They seemed to be arguing about something.

Presently he heard a "thump, thump, thump" of heavy footsteps coming to the door of the room. He held his breath and prayed. Then came a "rap, rap, rap" on the door. The driver yelled, "Yeah!"

"You go ahead and have your fun with the kid. We're going into town to get some food. We'll get 'im later."

With that, they left the house and the door slammed behind them. Marlin heard the engine start and the car move on down the road. He looked at the driver seated with his chair propped against the door. He seemed to be half asleep, but Marlin didn't know what was going on with him. Suddenly he got to his feet and opened the door and looked out into the next room as if to make sure the others were really gone. He still seemed to be stoned or drunk. He sat down on the floor now, then stretched out and lay down in front of the door, tucking a filthy towel under his head for a pillow. Marlin took a deep breath and waited, not daring to move or speak. His mind was racing, and his heart pounded like a jack hammer.

In a matter of a minute or so, the driver was fast asleep. Marlin knew this was his only chance to escape, but how? He softly stepped to the window and checked to see if it was locked. The lock was broken but the sash was secured with two big nails. There was no way he could get it open. He took a deep breath and prayed again. In his heart, he asked God to forgive him for not paying more attention to his mother's instruction from the Bible. I really need your help now, Lord, he thought. More than I have ever needed you before; and I have been in some tight places. What should I do?

ESCAPE!

The driver stirred and began to snore. Marlin stepped back a few steps from the window, hesitated only a second and made a swift, powerful leap, crashing through the glass feet first. He fell to the ground but jumped up and ran as fast as he could go. He glanced back to see the driver climb out the broken window and start after him.

He darted this way and that, through the weeds, trees and bushes. He dodged low hanging limbs and tripped over dead branches. Vines and weeds caught him, causing him to fall, time and again, but he bounced back up and kept going. His heart pounded and he had trouble breathing. He didn't know which direction to run. He only knew that he must run. He must escape!

The thick underbrush made it difficult, but he couldn't give up. He fell beside a huge fallen tree. He rose to a sitting position, panting hard. Slowly, carefully, he raised his head and peered over it, looking for his pursuer. He caught a glimpse of him, struggling, stumbling through the weeds, but going at an angle away from him. Marlin relaxed and took a minute to catch his breath, until he heard the car returning up the road. He jumped to his feet again and ran!

Shortly, he heard the voices of the two men yelling at the driver, cursing, and calling him vulgar names. Then they joined him in the search for the boy. Their prey had escaped and they were furious.

Marlin was lost now, his sense of direction completely scrambled from all the confusion and fright he had experienced. He kept going straight ahead, away from the house he had left and hopefully away from the three men who had kidnapped him. Soon he came upon a narrow trail, worn there by the hooves of animals. This gave him new hope as he knew it could mean a residence was near, or perhaps a watering place for livestock. Either way, he was thirsty enough to drink from a cattle tank full of green slimy moss, if necessary. He followed the trail, looking over his shoulder often to make sure no one was behind him. As he reached the top of the hill, he could see a farmstead below. He felt sure that would be a place of refuge. He said aloud, "Thank you, Jesus!"

Darting from tree to tree to avoid being seen, he was soon on the edge of the barn lot. From there, he hovered close to the rail fence, moving slowly until he reached the open door of the barn. He stepped inside and stood against the inside wall until he could breath easier and his eyes became accustomed to the semi darkness...

There was a huge stack of hay, a tractor and other implements, but no livestock. The sweet smell of the hay reminded him of home, of a happy time when it was only his mother and himself on a small acreage where they kept a horse, a cow and a few chickens. How he longed for the security and comfort of his mother's arms! But that would never be his to enjoy again.

Marlin became more aware of his thirst now. He had not had anything to drink since he and the Sheriff had eaten lunch. It seemed so long ago, but was only a few hours. Still, it was long enough to have a powerful thirst. He began to look for a cattle tank or windmill or something. Maybe there is a hydrant inside the barn, he thought. Looking around, he saw one just outside the door on the opposite side from which he had come in. Cautiously, he stepped out to it and turned it on. He cupped his hands and bent to drink the cool refreshing liquid. He rubbed some into his hair and washed his face.

Should I go and knock on the door or stay out of sight? He returned to the barn and sat down near the haystack, to relax. He hadn't realized how dreadfully tired he was until now. He closed his eyes, his head began to nod, and soon he was fast asleep.

GOOD COUNTRY FOLKS

When he opened his eyes again it was pitch dark. He had no way of knowing what time it was, but he knew it was night. He closed his eyes again and slept.

As the sun began to peek over the horizon, a perky rooster began to crow loudly, awakening Marlin. He sat up and rubbed his eyes. Where am I? He wondered. Then he remembered.

Stretching, he became aware of his empty stomach growling. He got up, stretched, and looked out the door toward the farm house. The lights were on now as the residents were up and ready to start their busy day. As he stood in the barn doorway, a man suddenly appeared from behind a truck nearby. He saw Marlin and walked quickly toward him. Marlin went to meet him. He remembered his little speech he had prepared yesterday.

He stretched out his hand and began, "Hello Sir. My name is Marlin Morris...."

Before he could finish the man interrupted with "What were you doing in my barn?"

"I'm sorry Sir," Marlin replied. "Actually, I slept there by the haystack. I hope you don't mind, but I had no place to go. I was in a heap of trouble and ran in there to hide, and then fell asleep."

"What kind of trouble are you in? Is the law after you?"

"Oh no, Sir," Marlin replied. Plunging his hand into his pocket he handed the Sheriff's calling card to the man saying, "This man is a friend of mine. You can call him and ask about me. He told me to call him anytime I needed him, but I have no way to call."

"Who were you running from, then? Who were you hiding from?"

"Oh boy, that is a story I hope you will believe." He told the whole story, beginning with the death of his mother and ending with his bed in the barn.

"All right, kid. It does sound far fetched, but somehow I tend to believe you. Come on into the house and have some breakfast while I call the sheriff. If your story is true, those three hoodlums are probably wanted by the law."

The man stopped at the porch and offered his hand, saying, "My name is Goodwin. Charles Goodwin." Marlin grasped his hand firmly and answered with,

"Marlin Morris is my name."

Mr. Goodwin opened the door and held it for Marlin to enter. Mrs. Goodwin turned in surprise to see Marlin there with her husband.

"Diane, this is Marlin Morris. Marlin, my wife, Diane"

Marlin stepped forward and offered his hand to her. "And where did you find him?" She asked her husband with a smile.

"I found him in the barn."

"*You found him in the barn?*"

"Yes. It's a long story. Just give him something to eat, will you? I need to make a phone call. I'll eat in a few minutes."

He moved to the office in the back room and closed the door.

Mrs. Goodwin had already set the table for four, and now added another place setting for Marlin. "Sit here, Marlin. I will call the kids to join you. They are getting ready for school."

She stepped to the foot of the stairs and called, "Kendra! Mark! Breakfast is ready!"

The two youngsters quickly descended the stairs, then stopped short at seeing this stranger seated at their table.

"Kids, this is Marlin. Marlin, this is Kendra and Mark, our children. Go ahead and sit down, kids, and have your breakfast. Your Father will be in shortly. He will fill in the details about Marlin when he returns. The bus won't wait, you know!"

The children were a little younger than Marlin, and seemed hesitant to sit with him, but his friendly smile and quiet way soon won them over and they began to chatter and eat their breakfast. Mr. Goodwin returned to the room with a pleased expression on his face.

"The sheriff verified your story, Marlin. I'm sure glad he did. I had my doubts at first. Have you met the kids?"

Everyone responded in the affirmative. "I'm sure you are all curious about the guest I brought in today. You won't have time to hear his whole story before you leave for school, so let me just tell you, he is okay. He may be here for a few days until we can help his sort some things out. He can tell you about himself this afternoon when you get home. Your bus is here now!"

The two children quickly gathered their book bags, kissed their mother and father good-bye and rushed out the door.

"I hope *I* don't have to wait until afternoon to hear your story, Marlin. I'm dying of curiosity!" Mrs. Goodwin said with a smile. Resting her chin on her hands she looked expectantly to Marlin.

Marlin glanced at Mr. Goodwin for approval before sharing his story with her. Then he began again to relate the whole episode. She listened intently .with tear filled eyes as she heard of his painful ordeal. Turning to her husband she asked, "What did the Sheriff say about those three hoodlums? Are they wanted by the law? If they weren't before, they should be now!"

"The sheriff said it sounded like the trio they have been looking for. If it is, they are wanted for several offences. From what Marlin told me, they are using the Kester place for a hide out. That's only a mile and a half from here, which is a concern for us, because of our kids. The sheriff's men are going to be over there today and try to arrest them. They will be calling back to keep us informed."

"I sure hope they catch them and the sooner the better!" she replied.

She began to clear the table and put the dishes in the dish washer. Marlin stacked the remaining dishes and carried them to her. As she took them from his hand, she said, "Marlin, I'm so sorry you have been through such heartache, and then to have these awful characters grab you.... It's just awful! I'm so glad you escaped. They might have killed you!"

"When Mother was alive, she used to try to teach me about God. I really didn't pay too much attention, I guess, but when this happened, I started thinking a lot about God. I was really praying for the first time in my life! I believe God heard me and helped me out. Otherwise, I *might be* dead by now."

Instinctively, she reached out and drew the boy to herself and hugged him tightly. He began to sob and clung to her. Tears flowed freely down her cheeks, falling onto his shoulder. After a few minutes they released the hug and stood with clasped hands, studying one another... A real bonding took place in that moment.

Smiling through his tears, he said, "Thank you, Mrs. Goodwin. That is the first hug I have had since Mama died." She quickly hugged him again, saying, "Well, it won't be the last!"

LONELINESS SETS IN AGAIN

Cox was experiencing conflicting emotions since Marlin left his house. He too had bonded with the boy and desperately wanted to help him find a suitable place to live. Having the kid around, even though for such a short time, had caused him to realize what he had missed by not being married and having kids. It awakened the fathering instinct in him and he didn't understand it. He had always kept busy to avoid thinking too deeply about much of anything meaningful.

Since moving here to this little shack, he hadn't made any close friends either. He had no one with whom to share his troubling thoughts. For reasons he couldn't understand, he *wanted* to tell someone his story. The story of why, at this stage of life, when he should have been married, with grown children and grandchildren, been living in a nice home, driving a good vehicle or two, owning a nice spread with good cattle, good fences and all that goes with it, here he was, living in a little shack, with no furniture. He was sleeping on a cot and hanging his few clothes on nails driven in the wall. He had a small radio that sometimes worked, and no television. There was no water piped into the house and no bathroom. His washing machine was a five gallon bucket and his two hands. The refrigerator was on its last legs, and he cooked on a hot plate. One advantage to being poor, he told himself, was that there were few bills to pay.

He felt like a total failure. He knew the neighbors must be talking about him and his strange circumstances. They had to wonder if he was a recluse, a hobo, or what.

The longing in his heart to express his feelings and to tell his story, drove him to do something he had never considered doing before. That is, to put the whole thing down in black and white. He went to a box in the corner, rummaged through it and brought to the table, a writing tablet and an ever sharp pencil.

As he sat thinking about just how to begin, he had to fight a whole range of emotions, including resentment, jealously, hatred, self doubt, and fear.

He needed a title for this biography, but what should it be? Tricked? Hood winked? Betrayed? Yes, that would do it. So he wrote across the top of the page in large letters:

BETRAYED

I grew up in a loving Christian home, with two brothers and one sister. We lived on a farm and cattle ranch near the border of South Dakota in Nebraska. I was very happy growing up. I didn't have a care in the world. My parents took care of everything. When I was enough, I was taught to work and help out. All of us worked together to make the place a success.

When I went to High School, I was well liked and made good grades. My parents were proud of me and my siblings. I graduated and went off to find a job. I wanted to try my own wings. I knew I could make it on my own. My parents encouraged me to try to find a ranch or farm near them so I could come home now and then. I liked that idea as I loved my parents and my home.

I had been riding a horse since I was 'knee high to a grasshopper' and Dad had given me a good, cow horse, so I rode off into the sunrise one spring morning, whistling and twirling my lariat rope. I was full confidence as I rode along the dusty country roads. I had my bedroll tied behind my saddle, a canteen of water, and a big lunch. What more could a boy want?

The slogan, "Go west, young man, go west" stuck in my mind, so I rode west. On the fourth day, about a hundred miles from home, I found a ranch hand out checking fence. As we talked he told me of a place on up the road that needed a ranch hand.

When I arrived, they were busy in the corral, branding and working calves. I asked if they needed any help. The rancher invited me to join in and they would see if I knew anything about ranch work. I went right to work and they were pleased with what I did. They hired me, gave me a bed in the bunk house and my dreams began to come true.

I worked for that ranch for five years and enjoyed every day of it. They treated me right and fed me real good. Then one day, their son, who had been away at college, came home, and I was out of a job. They gave me a bonus along with my regular pay, and I was on the road again. I decided to go home, as it had been several months since I had seen my family.

Riding along, I met another cowboy who claimed to be looking for work, so we rode together and talked about life, work, family and our dreams for the future. He was my age and about my size. Actually, we looked a lot alike, for not being relatives.

At first, I liked the guy, but as time went on, I began to wonder about him. His stories didn't ring true. His experience of working on ranches seemed to be embellished, to say the least. I began to think he didn't know one end of a cow from another, but I kept quiet about it. I was about half way home when he invited me to join him for a few drinks at the local pub. He said he knew the little town coming up and had friends there. I had never been a drinker, but reluctantly agreed to go along. He said his friends would give us a place to sleep that night.

We entered the pub just as it was getting dark. The crowd was rowdy and the music was loud. He greeted his friends and they ordered drinks. I said I'd just have a coke. They hooted and laughed and made a big scene about it, trying to convince me to have a shot of bourbon. They yelled at the scantily dressed barmaid to bring me a shot. She brought it and began to sweet talk me, trying to get me to drink it. I insisted on the coke, which she finally brought and placed in front of me.

I watched the commotion around me and wondered what I had gotten myself into. My head began to spin. I felt as if I were falling asleep and didn't know why. Then I must have blacked out because I was unaware of anything else until a couple of police officers snapped hand cuffs on my wrists and began to shove me into a squad car.

At the police station, they fingerprinted me, and threw me into a jail cell. They said they would be back when the liquor had worn off. I tried to tell them that I had had nothing to drink, and they said, "Yeah, that's what they all say," and slammed the steel door shut with a loud bang.

I could not stay awake! The next morning, I awoke with a throbbing headache! I felt for my wallet, remembering the nice "nest egg" I had there. It was gone! I had no money, no identification; even the loose change I had carried in my pocket was gone. I glanced at my wrist and saw that my watch was gone too! I began to panic. *What is happening? Why am I in jail? I knew I had done nothing illegal!*

I heard the click, click, click, of someone's heels coming toward the cell door. A key was inserted in the lock, turned, then the heavy door opened and a uniformed officer entered. He began to read me my rights.

Later, I found myself sitting in a small room with an investigator who was asking me all kinds of questions about where I was on the night of such and such day. I insisted that I was at work or at the bunkhouse on the Norton ranch, but he didn't accept that answer. It went on and on endlessly. Finally the investigator stood to his feet and pointing his finger in my face said in a loud voice, "I know you are lying, and we will get the truth out of you one way or the other!"

I was left speechless. *What good does it do to tell them the truth fifty times, when they refuse to believe it forty nine times? I was completely frustrated, confused and angry. Wasn't I still in America? The good, free country, where truth always wins? What is going on here?*

Another officer took over and began again. "Where were you on the night of....?"

I lost my temper. I stood and began to yell "What about my right to make a phone call? You throw me in jail; ask the same questions over and over until I am sick to death of it. You won't believe me when you could easily check it out. You have taken my wallet, my money and even my watch, and you haven't even told me why I am in here!"

Then I collapsed in the chair and let my head fall to the table and cried like a baby.

The officer quietly watched, saying nothing. Finally, he said, "Okay Patrick, lets go back to the cell."

I told you, Sir. My name is not Patrick, I yelled at him. It is Weston Cox. Please, let me call my father. He lives down by Trenton. He will verify everything I've told you."

It was no use. They put me back into the same cell again and slammed the door shut.

In the days, weeks and months to follow, I was never given a chance to call my parents. I couldn't help wondering if they had any idea where I was and why. I was satisfied that they didn't.

Years later I learned from my brother what took place while I sat rotting in jail;

When they hadn't heard from me for several months, Dad called the Norton ranch to ask about me. He learned that I had left to go home five months earlier. He became concerned, knowing I would have let them know if I had taken a job on another spread along the way. He began to drive back along the roads, stopping at every home in sight and ask people if they had seen me.

Near the little berg they call Paxton, where we had gone to the pub, someone told him about seeing two young cowboys riding along together toward Paxton. He went there asking questions. He was told that one of the cowboys, by the name of Patrick had been arrested on suspicion of armed robbery and murder and was still in jail at the county seat. The other one had taken both their horses and ridden off alone.

Dad determined to go to the jail and talk to this "Patrick." Maybe he would give him some information as to where I had gone. When he went to the Police Department and requested to speak to the guy, they refused to allow it. They did show him a picture and the rap sheet showing the charges that were being filed. It was actually a picture of Patrick Blumfield. Dad was satisfied, that at least I was not in jail.

During the months following, I was brought to trial and convicted of murder in the commission of the crime of armed robbery. Dad knew that I would have gone on home with the horses, if the second cowboy was me, so what could possibly have happened to me? He decided at that moment that he would spend all his money and his time to search until he found me. He went home and told Mother. My siblings were gone from home now and on their own. It was only the two of them left to run the farm and take care of the cattle.

They talked it over and agreed to sell out and move to a small place to save money.

After the auction, they found a little house on the outskirts of Mainard, Nebraska, and began the long investigation and search for their missing son. They checked the ranches and farms, one by one. He asked if they had they hired any new cowboys in the last year? Who are they? If they had one about my age, they asked to meet him. They would then ask whether they might have seen me. They looked at the ranch horses, hoping to find "Sox" on whom

I had ridden away from home. They checked all the saddles, knowing that they would recognize mine if they saw it. It was a slow and painful process for them but they would not give up. I was their son!

Out of desperation, they hired a private investigator, believing in his expertise, but he proved to be a big disappointment and cost a lot of money. The months dragged by, taking a severe toll on my parents. Dad had a serious heart attack in the fifth year of my forty year sentence. His medical expenses almost finished depleting his funds before he passed away. Mother was so stressed by it all that her health began to fail as well. Within two more years, she was gone. Of course, I knew nothing about any of this. I had no contact with the outside world. I was completely cut off. When I wrote letters, they apparently were discarded. I never got a reply to any of them. I felt so alone and abandoned. I lived one day at a time, mostly without any hope.

Eventually, I was released when the real Patrick Blumfield made a deathbed confession to the crime and explained how he had switched identities with me and let me take his rap. He was from a rich, influential, family, who had managed to manipulate the legal system and keep me isolated and locked up all these years instead of their own son.

Upon my release, I returned to the home place to find new owners in charge and everything changed. It was no longer my home. I was heartsick and confused! Where are my parents? I had been away twenty eight, long, miserable years, and now I was homeless, and unable to find my dear parents. I began to search for them just as they had searched for me.

I hitch- hiked along the once familiar roads until I found a former neighbor, who still lived on his place, I hoped. At least his name was on the mailbox. When I knocked at the door, he shuffled across the room and opened it. I didn't recognize this white haired gentleman before me.

"Are you Joe Carter?

"Yes, I am." He leaned heavily on his cane and seemed to have difficulty breathing. He was so different from the strong, vigorous man I knew as a youngster. Of course I had to introduce myself. He seemed to be totally dumfounded when I told him I was Weston Cox.

"You're Weston Cox?" He yelled. "That's impossible! How can you be Weston Cox? He's been gone for nearly thirty years. His parents spent all their life's earnings and died, trying to find him, and now you show up claiming

30

to be him?" He seemed angry, as if I had done something evil against my parents.

"My parents are dead?" I asked. I couldn't grasp the meaning of his words. "My parents are dead?" I asked again. Then I began to cry like a little orphaned boy. Mr. Carter softened and urged me to come in and sit down. After a few minutes, I regained my composure and asked, "When? How? Please tell me everything you know."

"First, you tell me where you have been all these years. Then I'll think about telling you about your folks," he said gruffly.

I hesitated to tell him, knowing how unbelievable it sounded to anyone who had never been in such a situation as this, but I did tell him and showed him the papers I carried as evidence. He studied them for a long time, as his eyesight was nearly gone. Still doubting, he dragged a chair over in front of me so he could look me in the face while he spoke.

It was a long, difficult story. It was difficult for him to tell, as he had been a dear friend of my family, and difficult for me to hear. I would never have knowingly brought them such heartache and distress. When he finished he was quiet for some time, wanting to give me time to absorb all the information. Then he said, "What a sorry, awful thing, to lose twenty eight years out of your life, and to think about what your folks suffered, by not ever knowing what happened to you."

I finally came to my senses enough to ask about his wife. She had been gone four years. He said he would never get used to it. I could see the effects of her absence here in the house.

I asked about my siblings. He said my sister had married a local guy and lived a few miles west of our place. I determined to go and visit her.

Joe had a telephone now and invited me to call her. It felt very strange, using a telephone after such a long time. She couldn't believe her ears. How could it be me after all these years? I asked Joe to talk to her. After awhile she believed me and wanted to come in the car and pick me up immediately.

We had a wonderful, tearful, reunion. She hardly took time to fix lunch for her hungry husband. She filled me in on all the news about the rest of the family, who each one married, how many kids they had, etc. etc.

She drove me to the cemetery where Mom and Dad are buried. It was overwhelming to read their names engraved on the marble headstones. I felt so

31

much guilt over their deaths, yet so helpless, and hopeless. Loneliness engulfed me again. I had not cried so much since they had convicted me of murder!

Sis tried to comfort me but, I was beyond reach at that point. We returned to the car and to her place. I spent several days there while she called our brothers and told them my story. They were anxious to see me, which was a great comfort to me.

Being reunited with the others helped my loneliness, temporarily, at least. Seeing their children and grandchildren was a joy, but it also increased my resentment toward the legal system of the country for taking away so much of my life and destroying my hopes and dreams. Here I was, past middle age, penniless, unmarried, with no home, and no future. And I had done nothing to deserve it!

Cox put his pencil down, stood up and stretched. He gazed out the small window thoughtfully for a few moments. He wondered why he had decided to write his story in the first place, after such a long time. He did seem to feel better for it, though. There was something therapeutic in putting it on paper. He didn't know whether anyone would care to read it or whether he would even want them to, but he wanted to finish it anyway, sometime.

He went out to check his few cattle. It gave him a great deal of satisfaction to finally have the freedom to come and go as he pleased and to own a few head of cattle. Maybe it wasn't too late after all, to fulfill his dream of having a ranch. He was fifty one years old, but in good health yet.

Since Marlin had come knocking on his door, his whole attitude toward life had changed. Until then he had not allowed himself to hope, and to dream. He wanted to find out where the kid was, and to do what he could for him. He didn't want this young boy's life to end up the way his had. It is more dangerous now than twenty eight years ago. Anything can happen out there. It is a new generation, a new time, a different kind of culture.

"I need to do what my folks did," he said aloud. "I need to go and search for that boy."

As he watched the cattle grazing contentedly, a plan began to form in his mind. He would take one section of ground each day, stop at every home, every abandoned shack, stop every vehicle, until he was sure Marlin wasn't there, then he would go to the next one.

He had to ask himself, what will you do if you find him? The sheriff had said he dropped him off on the north side of Allentown, so the sensible place to start would be right there. The Sheriff was from Buckley. Perhaps I should contact him first. He may have some information about his whereabouts. Cox wished he had a telephone. It was the first time he had really thought about it. But how would he pay for it? He had borrowed money from his brothers to buy this sorry little place and the cows. His brother in law had given him the pickup truck, and he was trying to live on the little he had left from the loan until he could sell the calves. He decided he would drive over to the Black's place and borrow their telephone.

Once he returned to the house, the story he was writing caught his attention again. He sat down and began another chapter.

I borrowed enough money from my brothers to get a little place near Cameron and to buy some pregnant cows to put on it. I had a lot of work to do on the fences and pastures, so that kept me occupied for awhile. The little shanty of a house wasn't much but it sure beat the heck out of a prison cell! It had electricity and a little house out back big enough for "business "as well as some gardening and fencing tools. Now I could enjoy the open air and the fruit of my labor. I began to heal. I had lived for several years on hope, and then gave up hope. Then I lived on hatred. I hated the system that did this to me and the people who let it happen. After that I began to blame God. I became an atheist. That belief system was strong in the prison. There were plenty of books on it and people coming to speak in favor of it. But after studying it, trying to believe it, even promoting it, I realized I was more miserable than ever, so I gave that up and went back to my roots. I began to seek God.

I am convinced that the only real satisfaction, the source of all joy, is in knowing God through his Son, the Lord Jesus Christ. I gave my heart fully to Him and the last ten years in prison actually became tolerable. Sometimes I was even happy. I had purpose in life. Once more, I had hope. I added faith to hope and eventually, I was set free and cleared of all wrongdoing, where the law was concerned. I like to say, "I was set free while in prison and then set free to get out!"

"That's enough for now. I have things to do." Once more he was talking to himself. Being alone causes one to do that, he reasoned. Leaving the driveway, he drove directly over toward the Black's ranch. They greeted him warmly and with many questions about Marlin. They gladly let him use the telephone. Cox became noticeably riled, then excited as he heard what had taken place with Marlin and what was going on concerning the three outlaws.

He repeated all the information to the Black family, explaining that the law had the Kester place staked out and was waiting for the three to return to their lair. They were confident that they would have them in custody very soon.

Cox was anxious to see Marlin again and to make sure he was being cared for. When he located the place, Marlin came running to meet him before he could get out of the truck. He opened the door and threw his arms around Cox's neck, laughing and crying at the same time. He was *so* glad to see him!

As they and the Goodwin family stood in the shade of the trees, getting acquainted and visiting, they heard a police siren screaming up the road in the distance. They all stood quietly, holding their breath, hoping this meant the arrest of the three men who were a threat to their security.

A short time later, the sheriff drove into the driveway with the good news they had hoped for. The three men were in custody and on their way to jail.

Mrs. Goodwin brought out iced tea and cookies and they had a little celebration. Then the sheriff called Cox aside to talk privately. He had done some investigating of his own, but not about the outlaws. It was about Weston Cox. He knew all about the mistaken identity, the wrongful conviction, the years Cox had spent in prison as well as the death of his parents.

"Mr. Cox, I'm here to tell you how sorry I am for the injustice you have suffered at the hands of crooked men in the system who apparently took bribes to keep you locked up all those years. I'm also here to tell you that you have the right to bring a lawsuit against them and be repaid a good deal of money for all you have suffered."

"I appreciate you saying that, but I wouldn't know where to begin. I am afraid of ending up in prison again just for challenging the system."

"Don't worry about that. We have a group of attorneys in this area that have volunteered to take care of this for you, free of charge. They just need your permission. They have been watching this case for a long time and are anxious to see it set straight."

"I don't know, Sheriff. I'm very nervous about dealing with the law. You understand my misgivings, don't you? As much as I need some money and would like to see the rascals pay for what they have done..."

"I give you my word, Cox. I'll go with you and oversee everything they do. I'll read all the paper work, including the fine print. I want to see you reimbursed for the time you have lost, even though I know you can't really be compensated for your ruined life."

The two men studied one another for some time. Cox was struggling with internal conflict: The fear, the hope of a new start, the mistrust of the legal system, and the desire for justice kept him in turmoil. He didn't know whether it was worth the risk. Still, he had this good man here, promising him help, giving him assurance.

"If you need time to think about it, I understand. I'll come by and see you the day after tomorrow. I have business out that way anyhow. Will that be all right?"

"Yeah, that would be great. I do need to think it over. Thank you so much!" They shook hands warmly and the sheriff left, while Cox returned to the little party on the lawn.

THINGS ARE LOOKING UP

Cox stood quietly watching the interaction between the Goodwin family and Marlin. He could see that they had come to a mutual respect. Marlin seemed to fit right into the family. He was pleased about that. If he couldn't take him in, then this was the best outcome he could wish for. That is, if they wanted to continue to keep him.

Mr. Goodwin walked over to where Cox stood leaning against a tree, drinking tea. "Cox, would you like to go along with me to check on a cow I have penned up? She is ready to calve so I'm keeping an eye on her."

The two men walked directly toward the barn, matching stride for stride. They had a lot in common it seemed, although Mr. Goodwin had no idea about Cox's past.

"I wanted a chance to talk to you away from the family," said Mr. Goodwin. "I get the impression from Marlin that you two are very close. Is that right?"

"I really haven't known the kid but a few days, but I do care a lot for him. Why do you ask?"

"Well, my wife and I have talked it over and we are willing to keep him around, give him a home, send him to school this fall, and see that he is treated right, but we don't want to come between him and a good buddy like yourself."

"Charles, I think that is wonderful of you. I don't have any right to him and certainly wouldn't interfere with such an opportunity as you are offering. If I had a place for him and the money to do what he deserves, I would have already made that offer, but I don't have. Maybe in the future I could take him. Right now, I can't promise anything."

"Here's the cow. Well look at that! She's already had the calf and is nursing it! That's what I like to see."

"Yes, it does give a guy a great deal of satisfaction to see a young heifer who is such a natural mother."

The men leaned over the rail fence watching the cow and calf for a few minutes. Continuing the discussion, Mr. Goodwin asked; "Are you sure you are all right with us keeping him then?"

"Yes, of course I am."

"Let's keep in touch about this. It could be that you'll be able to take him in a year or two. That might be something we both should consider. My kids will be ready for college before too many years. Marlin is older than they are. It would be good if he could go to college. It's hard to say what this economy will do by that time, but maybe one or the other of us could help him out. He's smart and responsible. He will do all right, what ever he decides."

"I agree, and I will do what I can. Sometime I will tell you my story so you will know why I am so destitute at this point in time. It's a long, painful story, and I don't share it with just anybody." Charles studied him quizzically but allowed him privacy concerning his life situation.

After saying good-bye to the family, Cox drove slowly up the road. He deliberately drove past the Kester place which had served as a hide out for the three suspects. It was nearly covered up with vines, scrub trees and weeds. He pulled his vehicle onto the barely visible road leading to the back of the house. It was kind of unnerving, just knowing what almost took place there. He parked the truck and went to try the door. It opened with a loud squeak of the hinges. His curiosity was aroused as he pushed the sagging door open wider. It scraped across the floor, where it had worn an arc from its dragging.

He stepped slowly across to the doorway leading into the kitchen. The place was strewn with paper plates, empty plastic bags, food scraps and all kinds of trash. It was dusty and musty. It smelled of rodents. Hearing a squeak, he glanced down just in time to see a large rat peeking out at him from a hole in the baseboard. He stomped his foot and the rat disappeared. Cox chuckled and continued through the house.

The kitchen had once been a beautiful room. The cupboards were still intact except for a couple of doors and a drawer front, lying on the floor. The sink was in good condition and the faucets, although dirty, looked okay. Cox was surprised to see that the floors were level, for the most part.

He went through the entire house. It was like the typical three bedroom house of its era. There were three bedrooms, a bathroom, which was a disaster, a living room and a dining room. The roof had been leaking for some time allowing the floor in the dinning room to become damaged.

Cox couldn't help but wonder why a house with so much promise had been abandoned and left to deteriorate like that. He would have to ask Mr. Goodwin about the history of the Kester family.

He closed the door behind himself and continued toward home. He had a lot to think about. Did he dare to dream? He decided he would make a trip to see his siblings again soon. He wanted their opinion about what was going on in his life. But the Sheriff was coming by and he had to be here for that.

It was spring, and school would be out soon. The Goodwin children were excited about that. They always enjoyed summertime at home with their parents and the trips they would take to see the grandparents. They enjoyed sight- seeing, fishing, swimming and all the fun things families do together. It was decided that Marlin would wait and start school in the fall, since the year was nearly gone anyway. In the meantime, he would help Mr. Goodwin around the farm.

"I'll tell you what, Marlin. Just call me Charles. I can't get used to being called "Mister." That will put us on more even ground, if you don't mind?"

"That suits me just fine, Mr. ah, I mean, Charles."

So the day began with the pair checking fence, repairing equipment, tilling the garden, etc. Charles was very impressed with Marlin's ability as well as his attitude. He was a good worker and didn't complain at all. Besides that, he was polite and appreciative. He asked himself, "Is this kid for real?"

After doing his few chores, Cox sat down and picked up his pencil again.

My life seems to be taking a turn for the better now. When I bought this little place, I thought it would do me for the rest of my life. I didn't have much to live for, anyway. But now, if I dare to dream, I may have a chance to have some money to do bigger, better things.

I may even have a chance to adopt a boy and call him "Son." I might have a decent house with running water and an indoor bathroom. I could have a closet for my clothes and clothes for my closet. Owning a pair of cowboy boots like I had when I was a kid at home or working on the Norton Ranch would be a thrill to me now.

There are some good people in this world. I have met several of them just recently. I am beginning to feel very blessed. That is a new feeling for me. I want to forgive all the hurts of the past and begin anew. I am a fairly old man to make a new beginning, but with the help of the good Lord, I can do it! I feel young today, almost like the day I left to find my first job. I feel like whistling and twirling my lariat rope!

The Sheriff's car rolled into the driveway about 1:00 o'clock. Cox had been watching for him, and immediately opened the door for the sheriff to enter. He came in carrying a folder stuffed with legal papers.

He began to lay them out in rows on the table, explaining to Cox what each one was and what needed to be done. The two men sat across the table from one another for two hours, discussing the court procedures, the risks, the attorneys fees, the time frame they should expect it to take, etc.

Then it was decision time. Cox sat thoughtfully studying the papers before him. He asked many questions. Some of them, the sheriff couldn't answer, so he made notes and promised to find someone who could. He waited for Cox to make up his mind what he wanted to do.

"I'll tell you what I would like to do, Sheriff. I'd like to go visit with my brothers and my sister about this before I decide. I have been out of "circulation," so to speak, for so long I don't know what is what anymore. They will know more about this thing. It won't take but a couple of days, and then I'll be a lot more confident about making the decision. What do you think?"

"You know, Cox, that is a wise thing to do. I don't blame you at all. This will wait. You go ahead and take all the time you need. In the meantime, I'll be checking with the attorneys group and see if they have any more advice for us."

So it was settled, and the sheriff left while Cox checked the oil, etc. in the truck and made the necessary preparations for the cows for a couple of days. He would leave early the next morning.

GETTING ACQUAINTED

With her own children in school during the day, Mrs. Goodwin had time to spend alone with Marlin. She had already done some shopping and bought him some clothes. She really enjoyed the boy. It was evident that he had had some good instruction in manners, showing appreciation and responsibility. He was always quick to help with any little thing, from the dishes to sweeping the floor or outside chores. He enjoyed the time he had with Mr. Goodwin as well.

Mrs. Goodwin was interested in knowing more about his past, so one day as they worked together in the kitchen, she asked him, "Marlin, I know this might be painful for you, but I'd like to hear about your early years. Do you remember what it was like when you were just a little tyke? What was your mother like? What kind of things did you enjoy doing together?"

Marlin was thoughtful for a moment, and then he began: "Of course I wasn't there when they got married, but she told me about it so many times that it seems like I was. I have the picture in my mind like a movie. She said it was a beautiful day in June of 1985. The little church was packed with people who had come to hear them say their vows and see the bride and groom. They had both grown up in Buckley and everybody knew them.

When the wedding was over, they had a party for them with gifts and cake and punch. All the women were telling Mother how beautiful she looked and how handsome Dad was. Then they went on a short trip together and had lots of fun.

When they got back they went to live on Dad's little place in the country. He had bought twelve acres and built a house on it before they

41

got married. Then he bought a cow and a horse and some chickens. He worked hard to build shelter for all of the critters, as he called them, before cold weather set in.

They were very happy there. Dad had a job in a factory and would be gone most of the day, so when he came home, Mom had a nice meal for him. She took care of the animals except on week ends. He wanted to do it then.

Before long, I was on the way. They were very excited about that and began to fix up the nursery. But before I was born, a drunk driver ran a stop sign and hit Dad's car, killing him instantly.

Mother was heartbroken. All her dreams were destroyed. People were so good to her, though. They helped her get through the funeral, and then I was born and they helped her with me.

She always told me that I looked just like my dad! She said having me helped her get over the pain of losing Dad, but she was very lonely.

When I was big enough to walk, she would take me out and let me chase the chickens, get the eggs out of the nests, and play with the cats and the dog. She used to put me on the horse and lead him around. I barely remember that first horse. Then he died. Mother didn't have the money to buy another horse, so we didn't have one for a long time. Then a friend of hers gave us one. It was an old horse that walked funny. Something was wrong with his feet, but he was okay for me to ride, since I was small.

I was about five years old and I didn't realize how hard it was on Mother to be alone so much. We always went to church on Sunday and usually spent time with friends all afternoon. She liked people, so she was happier when there were more people around.

Then one day, this strange man began to come to our house to see Mother. He would take us to a movie or we would pack a picnic lunch and go to a nice spot down by the creek and sit on the ground to eat. I could tell that he liked Mother a whole lot and I didn't like it when she started liking him too. I guess I was jealous.

"Is he the one who became your step- father?" She asked.

"Yes. One day, I think it was when I was six years old they told me that they were going to get married and that I would have a new dad. "Wouldn't that be wonderful?"

"Well, I didn't like the idea. I wanted our life to stay the same, with only Mom and me. But when I was at school one day, they went someplace and got married. He moved into my house and started bossing me around. That caused a lot of arguments between them. Mom didn't like the tone of voice he used with me and he was the same way with her sometimes. I started wondering why he had changed so much. He used to be nice to us and now that they were married he was getting mean. I thought it must be my fault so I tried real hard not to make him mad."

"Did he hit you, Marlin?"

"Not at first. He just yelled. Then he started calling me names."

"What kind of names?"

"He called me stupid, good for nothing, dummy, and stuff like that."

Marlin was quiet for a moment, his brows furrowed as he remembered those difficult times. Then he spoke again; "After that, he started yelling, cussing and calling me real bad names. Mother would be crying and begging him to stop, but he wouldn't. He started yelling at her. Then one day he hit her and told her to shut her _____ mouth or he would knock her teeth out. I was so scared! I knew that he would do it too, so I ran and threw my arms around her and begged her not to say anything. I didn't want him to hit her again."

"And did he hit her again?"

"Not that day, but one day when I got off the school bus, she was sitting on the porch crying. Her face was all bruised and her lip swollen, and bloody. I said, "Mother, what happened?" She shook her head and wouldn't answer me. I felt sick in my stomach. I knew he had beaten her up. I started planning how I could kill him for hurting my mother."

"Where was he at that time?"

"I think he had gone to town to the liquor store. I learned later that he had a problem with liquor."

"Did you talk to your mother about the thoughts you were having?"

"Yes, I did tell her. She was real worried then. She begged me not to do anything like that. She explained that I would be in awful trouble and would be in jail forever. She said that would hurt her a lot worse that Bert hitting her. I never wanted to hurt Mother...."

"How old were you at that time, Marlin?"

"I was probably about nine. I figured out that if I could stay away from him, especially when he had a bottle, there wouldn't be as much trouble. He still would hit Mother sometimes, though. Then one day she got really sick. She was hurting so bad in her stomach that she walked like this- (He bent over with his face toward the floor.) Bert got her in the car and took her to the Doctor."

"I went to school, and rode the bus back home, and they were not there. I got real scared. Bert wouldn't let me use the telephone when he was home, but I got the phone book and found the number for the hospital. I ask if they had a Carol Simpson there. After awhile Mother said "hello." She could hardly talk loud enough for me to hear her.

She said she was very sick but she would be all right. She told me to take care of the critters until she got home. Then she asked me to be real extra good and not make Bert mad so he wouldn't yell at me. I promised I would do that."

"Did that work for you, Marlin?"

"No, it didn't work at all. He was madder and meaner than ever! He even blamed me for Mother being sick. He said it was my fault because I was such a sorry, good-for-nothing son that it made her sick. I cried myself to sleep every night thinking I was to blame for all the trouble that had come to our home."

"Did she get well enough to come home?"

"Yes, she did come home for a few months. Then she got sick again and went back into the hospital. It was awful trying to live with Bert. I avoided him all I could. Mother would be home for awhile, and then she would go back to the hospital. This happened so many times. I can't remember how many. Bert got meaner every time it happened. When she was home, he was hateful to her. I tried to take care of her as much as I could, but Bert didn't want me to. He would make me go outside away from her. I felt so bad for her. I loved my mother so much." The tears welled up in his eyes and began to trickle down his cheeks.

"Then one day the ambulance came for her. I thought she would probably die this time, and she didn't ever come home again. One day the telephone rang and I answered it because Bert was passed out on the couch. It was Mother. She asked me to come to the hospital to see her. She was very sick and wanted to see me and talk to me. She told me to

44

get permission to leave school and walk to the hospital the next day, so I did. When I found her room, it smelled very strange in there and she looked so white and sick I almost didn't know who she was. She smiled and reached for me. We hugged for a long time and we both cried."

"I'm sure it was hard for you to see her like that. Did she tell you good-bye then?"

"She let me stand up again so she could look me in the eyes. Then she told me she had to tell me something. "It will be very hard for you to hear, but I have to tell you," she said. That's when she told me she wouldn't be coming home again. She said she was going away to Heaven, to be with the Lord Jesus.""

At that point, he couldn't continue. He broke down crying again. Mrs. Goodwin held him in her arms and let him cry. She stroked his back and shoulders saying, "I'm so sorry, Marlin. I'm so sorry..."

Finally the sobbing subsided and he continued. "She tried to tell me this was not my fault, but Bert had pounded it into my head for so long that it was hard for me to believe that it wasn't. Do you think it was my fault, Mrs. Goodwin?"

"Of course it was not your fault! If it was anyone's fault, it was Bert's. But we can't put the blame on him for your mother's illness. Those things just happen sometimes. It seems like the best people are the ones who suffer the most. But she will never suffer any kind of way again, Marlin. Just remember that she is in Heaven with Jesus, where there is no more sorrow, or crying or pain. She will have nothing but joy and peace forever!"

"Thank you, Mrs. Goodwin. I needed to hear that from you."

"Tell me what happened after that day at the hospital."

"When I came home from school the next day, a friend of Mother's was waiting for me in her car. She came to meet me as I got off the bus. She put her arms around me and began to cry. I knew then, that Mother was gone. We went into the house and sat down on the couch together. Then she told me, "Marlin honey, your mother went to be with the Lord a while ago." I didn't say anything. I just looked at her for a long time. But I didn't see her. I was seeing something else..." His voice trailed off and he fell silent, lost in thought again, remembering that day.

"What did you see?" Diane asked gently.

"I saw angels. I saw Mother, floating away with them, and she looked so happy and peaceful. I wished I could go with them. I didn't want to be left here alone, with Bert. Mrs. Fowler saw Bert drive into the yard and said she had to go, so she excused herself and Bert came into the house. He just looked at me with hatred in his eyes. I went to my room and took off my good shirt because it was a hot day. I went out the back door and started feeding the chickens. Then he came out and yelled at me."

"What did he say?"

"He said, come here, knot head, so I walked over to him. That's when he told me that I no longer lived there, that it was *his* place, and if he ever saw me again, I was a dead duck! I didn't know what to do. Where would I go? I thought about my promise to Mother, that I would take care of the critters and be extra good. How was I going to do that? Then he reached for the ax that was leaning against the house and yelled, "Get! I mean now!" He ran at me with the ax above his head. I ran! I hid in the brush and cried for two days, and then I went on into Bucklin. I saw all the people going into the church. I watched them carry the casket in and knew it was Mother's. Then I walked to the cemetery east of town and hid in the bushes. I wanted to see where they were putting her. Finally they came and let the casket down into the grave. When it was out of sight, I began to run again. Finally I ended up at Mr. Cox's place.

THE COX FAMILY

Cox arrived at his sister Laura's place around 10:00 o'clock the nest morning. Both of his brothers, Chip and Rush, were waiting for him. They were anxious to hear what he had to say and also spend time with him. Too much precious time had been lost over the past years and they didn't want to lose any more.

After an affectionate welcome, they gathered around the large kitchen table for coffee and rolls. The house was warm and inviting. The aroma of the freshly baked cinnamon rolls still lingered in the air. The other family members gathered in the living room to play board games while the discussion took place in the kitchen.

Cox immediately laid out the papers the sheriff had brought him and explained what they were about. The three siblings all had more education than Cox did so he counted on them to help him understand all the procedures and help him with the decision.

They each picked up the various papers, reading and asking questions. After an hour had passed, they all agreed that Cox should file the lawsuit. They assured him that they would help any way they could. They all agreed that he deserved compensation for all the years he had wrongfully been locked up.

At noon, they had a wonderful meal together, and then he returned to his little house beside the road. He was excited now. This was the best hope he had had for many years!

He thought of going on into Bucklin, to the sheriff's office, but his past years of experience had left him with little confidence in that regard. He would just wait for the sheriff to come to him the next day. When he came, Cox was ready to sign the papers and get the ball rolling. They were both satisfied that everything was working out well.

After the papers were filed, there was nothing to do but wait and pray. Cox had been doing a lot of that lately. The first 18 years he was in prison, he had become hard and agnostic. Why would a good God allow an innocent man to be falsely accused and imprisoned all these years? He had allowed his mind to dwell on that thought until he became an unbeliever, or thought he had. He then realized he was on the wrong thought trail, so he repented and began to go the church services that were held there for the prisoners. He recommitted his heart to the Lord. Then after his release, his sister had given him their mother's Bible, well worn, tear stained, full of notes and underlined. He had been reading it, and his hard heart was beginning to soften. He remembered his upbringing; the church services, the family prayers and Bible reading. It had been a good, happy life. He couldn't forget the day he had gone forward in church and asked the Lord to forgive his sins and be his Savior. And the day he and his brothers were all baptized down in the swimming hole on the creek.

He tried to keep busy and be patient, but it was hard to do. Everything depended on the outcome of the lawsuit. He was so grateful to Sheriff Baker for his help, as well as the group of lawyers who were working on the case. Their investigation had revealed some startling facts about what had actually happened back then.

He decided to write these things into the story he had begun.

MORE FACTS REVEALED

In the year of 1972, when I left the Norton Ranch to return home, I met this guy by the name of Patrick Blumfield. I could never have imagined that this chance meeting would cost me twenty eight years of my life. As the investigation revealed, he had come from a very wealthy family but was out looking for fun and excitement. He joined up with a wild crowd and they begun to roam around the area, holding up quick shops, having drunken brawls and trying to elude the law, just for excitement. Their little game lost it fascination when the law began closing in on them, so they split up and each went his own way.

Patrick had always dreamed of living the romantic life of the cowboy as he'd seen in the movies. Now was the perfect opportunity. He ran his car out of oil and it quit, so he abandoned it in the woods and began to hitchhike from ranch to ranch, looking for a place to learn to ride. He came upon an old, run down place three hundred miles from his home town. He convinced the two elderly bachelor brothers who owned the place, that he was just a kid, down on his luck, and needed a job.

They felt sorry for him and took him in. They taught him to ride and tried to give him a fresh start as a cowboy. He repaid their kindness by stealing the horse and all the gear, and riding away in the night.

He was out of liquor money, but he still had his pistol and some ammunition, so that wasn't a problem. He went to the nearest liquor store, shot the proprietor and made off with the cash and a supply of whisky. He managed to elude the law long enough to consume the liquor and sleep it off. He slipped into a house and stole enough food to meet his needs for a few days, but the life of hiding out alone wasn't exciting enough. He saddled the horse one day and rode out on the trail seeking more mischief.

49

That's where I met up with him, much to my regret. He had bribed the barmaid to slip me a "mickey" in my coke and then exchanged my wallet with his, took all my money and my watch, then rode off on my horse, while leading the stolen nag.

He made it back to his parents' home, where they kept him hidden from the law. They hauled the two horses and saddles up into North Dakota and sold them to a rancher there. When they returned home, they got in touch with the judge and proceeded to pay bribes to the "powers that be" so that I was kept in jail, convicted and sent "up the river."

They took Patrick to a plastic surgeon in New York, and had his face changed, got him a new identification, and sent him on his way. He had lived all these years under an assumed name and managed to live a relatively clean life and keep out of trouble. Then when he fell ill with a brain tumor, his parents' money couldn't save him. That's when he decided to confess and I was finally set free. Penniless, and homeless, but free.

When I met Marlin, and then again, when I met Sheriff Baker, the world seemed to become a brighter, friendlier place. I feel as though I have walked out of a very dark cave into the sunlight. The sheriff has helped me get a lawsuit started that may give me a new start in life. If it is successful, I think I will try to start a little ranch of some kind where I can take young boys who are on the wrong road and help them to change directions. That would help me make something useful out of the years I have left on this earth. This is really a prayer. With God's help, we can do some good. Maybe Marlin will come here and help with it. He is a good example for youngsters to follow.

Cox left the house to go for a walk. He always felt more at peace with everything when he was out in the open air. He enjoyed the birds' singing, the leaves of the trees rustling, and watching the antics of the squirrels chasing one another up and down through the branches.

His thoughts seemed to be chasing one another, just like the squirrels. Tumbling, racing, crowding, and vying for the top spot in his mind. He thought about the house they referred to as the "Kester" place. How it had been so nice at one time and now was so neglected, yet had so much potential, a picture flashed across the screen of his mind that his life was

50

like that house. It had begun in the best way, with good Godly parents, siblings who were close and respectful, a nice place to live and learn responsibility and faith. Then suddenly, that jail door slammed shut on his life and it was changed forever. It became like the dirty, abandoned, rodent infested home, covered with vines and weeds. A place no one wanted. It was almost forgotten, but it still stood, square and solid, as if waiting for someone to care enough to give it another chance. Cox had now been given that second chance. He determined to make it worthwhile.

Returning to the yard, Cox started the truck and drove up the road to see Marlin and the Goodwin family. He brought his penciled story along. He figured they deserved to know what the facts were about his situation, especially since they were keeping Marlin.

He received a warm welcome at the door and was quickly ushered into the kitchen for coffee and cake. The children, Kendra and Mark, returned from school and came rushing into the house, excited about their school day. Charles was out checking the cattle, Mrs. Goodwin told Cox. He would be back shortly. Cox excused himself and went out to meet him near the implement barn.

Cox explained the purpose of being here so soon, but rather than have him read the story he had written, he decided to tell him the whole ugly tale. They leaned against the corral fence and talked for a good long while. Charles wagged his head and groaned as he heard what Cox had lived through.

"I never would have guessed. I'm sorry you had to go through that and for how many years? They kept you locked up for *twenty eight years?*"

"My reason for telling you this is not for sympathy. I wanted to tell you for Marlin's sake. I didn't tell him why I am so destitute and live in that little shack. I thought maybe you would tell him sometime. I don't want him to think I just didn't want to keep him or that I am lazy or have wasted my earnings on liquor or gambling or something."

"Sure, I'll tell him, whenever it seems right."

"Another chapter is being written to my story, Charles. Sheriff Baker said that I have the right to sue the system and the Blumfields for all this. He brought all the papers for me to sign. They even have a group of lawyers who donate their time and work to right some of these wrongs. They assured me that I could win this suit and have a good bit of money when it's over. I'm almost afraid to hope, but I signed the papers. They are working on it now."

"That's great, Cox! It could get you up on your feet again. At least it will help relieve some of the pain from the past, won't it? I hope you get a good settlement."

"If I get enough money to do it, I want to start a little ranch for troubled boys. With my experience I should be able to head them in the right direction."

"I think that is a wonderful idea, Cox. I will be praying for you. We need something like that. I know of three kids right now that could use that kind of place to live."

The two men walked slowly toward the house, talking seriously and thoughtfully about what this could mean for the future. They noticed another vehicle parked in the driveway.

"It looks like you have more company, Charles. I'll get out of your way and go on home."

"Now, hold on here, Cox. I know who that car belongs to. It's our neighbor, Mrs. Strong, from over the hill to the east. I want you to meet her. She lost her husband a year or more ago. She is a swell gal. You'll enjoy knowing her. Come on in here!" He held the door wide and Cox couldn't refuse.

The introductions were made and Mrs. Goodwin insisted that everyone stay for the evening meal. They were soon enjoying a good meal and uplifting conversation. Cox had not had such a pleasant time ever, that he could recall. He had been conveniently seated next to Mrs. Strong and had thoroughly enjoyed visiting with her. This was the first time since he was a young, free man that he had had any association with a woman and had convinced himself that romance was never going to be a part of his life experience. Suddenly, he was having second thoughts about that.

Marlin seemed to have adjusted to the family very well. He didn't wait for anyone to begin clearing the table, but quickly picked up the dishes and carried them to the kitchen himself. Kendra and her mother were on hand to finish the chore. It was good team work they seemed to enjoy.

All too soon, it was time to go. As they said good-bye, Mrs. Strong invited Cox to stop by and see her place. She had asked him if he needed some work. She had some repair jobs around the farm that needed a man's expertise. He was grateful for the opportunity to help her, so a time was set for it.

SHOTS FIRED!

Driving home, his heart seemed to be bursting! He had forgotten how exciting a woman could be. Every word that was spoken, every smile exchanged, was magnified in his memory with great pleasure, until **BANG!** His windshield shattered before his face! Instinctively he stomped the brake pedal and skidded to a stop. A car roared out from a side road and sped away.

Badly shaken, Cox was unable to collect his thoughts for a moment. He then realized someone had just tried to shoot him. The distinct bullet hole in the center of the broken glass proved that beyond any shadow of doubt, but he couldn't understand why, and didn't know what to do next. Living alone in his little house was no security. He couldn't even call for help, with no phone. What should he do? Where should he go?

He dared not return to the Goodwin's and put them in danger. Still shaking, he continued south, toward Bucklin. He would try to find Sheriff Baker. He was so thankful for the friendship of this man. He was beginning to be familiar with the town because of the trips he'd made here to discuss the lawsuit. But it was night now and he wasn't sure Sheriff Baker would be available. He still had trust issues and wanted someone he knew to talk with.

As he neared the sheriff's office he saw that same car whip around the corner in front of him. Now, this is serious, he thought. He hurried inside and was pleased to see Sheriff Baker as well as two other officers inside. As he began excitedly to explain what had happened, suddenly a bullet hit the large glass window of the building and became embedded in the wall behind the desk. Everyone dropped to the floor, then sprang up and ran to their vehicles to try to catch the assailant. Cox was left alone again, reeling with fright. Since he was already on the floor, he figured he would lay low until it seemed to be safe. The sheriff would surely return soon.

Sirens screamed in the distance. What had he gotten himself into this time? Could it be because of the lawsuit? Surely it couldn't be because of Marlin! His step father was mean and crazy, but Marlin couldn't be any threat to him now, could he?

Soon the sheriff did return. The two deputies were still in pursuit. Hopefully, they would be able to apprehend the person and they would find out what his purpose was in shooting at them.

They moved to an inner room to sit and try to relax while the sheriff wrote out a report on Cox's story of the incident. Their theory was that it was because of the lawsuit. It was the only logical explanation, if you could call it logical.

"Do you ever see or hear anything of Marlin's step- father?" Cox asked.

"I have seen him around the liquor store a time or two. That's about all."

"I can't help thinking that it's not right for him to get the place that rightfully belonged to Marlin and his mother." Cox said thoughtfully. "But I have enough trouble of my own right now. I don't want to start any for him."

"You know, I have been thinking about going to the courthouse and checking on just how that place is deeded. Mrs. Simpson may have been wise enough to have put it in her son's name or she could have had a pre-nuptial agreement. It could be that is why he chased the kid off."

Loud raucous voices and slamming of doors interrupted the conversation. The deputies entered, dragging the hand-cuffed stranger between them. They seated him in a chair and pulled out some equipment and began to fingerprint him. Eventually, he was placed in a jail cell for safekeeping.

The officers all gathered in the room where Cox was waiting anxiously for answers. They had forced the guy off the road and arrested him. In his vehicle, they found a hand- drawn map giving directions to Cox's place and ten thousand dollars wrapped in a paper with the words "Balance on completion."

"I didn't know I was worth $10,000.00," Cox quipped.

"Well, we have our work cut out for us with this case," the sheriff said. We'll have to prove it was Blumfield who hired the hit man. When we question him tomorrow, we may get some answers. If he confesses that it was, we will have to handle it perfectly to prevent Mr. Blumfield from getting off on some technicality. Turning to Cox he said, "I think it is safe for you to go home now, but I'll follow you out there just in case. I'd like to see you get a telephone installed. At least then you could call for help if you see something suspicious."

Cox drove away wondering how this would all turn out. "That guy sure knows how to spoil a pleasant evening, to say the least," he said aloud.

The sun was just beginning to peek over the horizon as he drove the truck into his driveway. He thanked the sheriff and stood watching him drive away. He had already missed a whole night's sleep so he figured he may as well get an early start on the day. He would do his chores and try to get a handle on his whirling thoughts and emotions. Maybe he would be tired enough to sleep tonight.

OL' SHEP

Driving back to town the sheriff thought about how completely alone Cox was out there. He needs a good watch dog, he thought. The department had a canine unit and he knew that they sometimes got a dog that didn't work out for them and they would adopt it out to some worthy person. He would check that out. If he could get Cox a dog, he would feel a lot more comfortable about the situation.

The next day, he drove to Cox's place with a nice German shepherd dog sitting in the car. Cox met him in the drive way. They discussed the case for a minute, and then Cox asked, "Where did you get the dog?"

"He was being trained for the canine unit but his temperament didn't fit, so they wanted to find him a good home. I thought you might take him. He will make you a good watch dog and a good companion. I even brought a bag of dog food."

"I love dogs and have wanted to get one, but honestly, I can't afford to feed one right now. I am thinking that I need to get a telephone first, and that's going to cost me more than I realized. I don't know how to manage it. The neighbor lady, Mrs. Strong, needs some work done, so maybe that will help."

"This dog really needs a home, Cox, so I'll tell you what. If you can't manage his feed bill, I'll keep him in dog food until you can. He's had all his shots; he's neutered, well trained and obedient. He'll make you a good dog, I guarantee. If it doesn't work out, I'll take him off your hands."

During the course of the conversation, Cox had been scratching the dog's ears and petting him. He was already beginning to like the dog. It was an offer he couldn't refuse.

He opened the car door for him to jump out, but the dog waited. "You'll have to give him the command to "come," the sheriff instructed.

"Come!" Before the word was hardly out of his mouth, the dog jumped out and stood next to Cox, watching his face, waiting for the next command. "Sit." Cox said. The dog sat. Cox chuckled. "I like that!" He said. "What is his name?"

"Oh, he has a real original handle. It's Shep." They both laughed.

"What else should I know about him? I don't want to mess him up."

They spent the next half hour going over the dog's training and commands. Cox was very impressed with Shep. The sheriff left and Cox and Shep walked around the whole place, so Shep would be familiar with the cattle and know that he should not bark at or chase them. When they returned, they drove to Mrs. Strong's place. The dog obediently sat in the truck while Cox spoke with Mrs. Strong. She noticed the dog and invited Cox to let him out, if he wouldn't get into any trouble.

As Cox worked, repairing fence, mending the barn door, etc. Shep was never more than a few feet away and watched everything. If a car drove along the road, Shep barked once, to warn Cox. When it drove on by, he relaxed again. "Good Boy!" Cox praised him. "You are going to be a big help and comfort to me, Shep."

At 12:00 o'clock sharp, Mrs. Strong appeared on the patio with a tray of food and lemonade, and called to him to come and "sit for a spell." As they ate and talked, Cox marveled at her knowledge of cattle and everything connected to that way of life. She told him that she loved country living and refused to move into town as her children had urged her to do.

She and her husband had reared six children, who had married and scattered from home. She missed having youngsters around. Cox thought she had kept herself in good shape and was attractive for her age. He hoped to get better acquainted, but right now, he had work to do.

At the end of the day, Cox knocked on the door again and reported that he had finished all the required tasks. She paid him for the day and asked if he would like to return in a few days and do more work. He gladly agreed on Friday morning.

Driving home, he talked to Shep about his day, his hopes and dreams and about what a good dog he was. It was good to have someone to talk to, even if it was only a dog.

Early the next morning, Cox and Shep made a trip into Bucklin again. He drove to the sheriff's office first, to find out if they had learned anything new about the shooting.

He was informed that they were having trouble getting any information from the shooter. They weren't even sure what his name was. He gave them the name of Kent Worthington, but they were doubtful about it. They hadn't found any matches for his finger prints in the files nor pictures in the mug shots that looked like him.

He and Sheriff Baker then went to visit with the attorneys who were working on the lawsuit.

"I'm glad to see you today," Attorney Wilkins said as they entered his office. "I have something I need to discuss with you." He ushered them into his inner office and invited them to sit down. He reached for some papers on his desk. "Mr. Blumfield was notified of the lawsuit being filed a couple of weeks ago, and today we received this offer from him." He handed Cox a paper, and waited while he read it, then handed it to Sheriff Baker. They exchanged a surprised look, and then asked the attorney, "Exactly what does this mean? He wants to settle out of court for only ten thousand dollars? Does he think 28 years out of a man's life is worth so little?"

"You have to understand, Mr. Cox. He is admitting guilt just by making the offer, but he knows very well that you are not going to settle for "peanuts." We will have to dicker with him to get it up there somewhere near where it belongs. He's got the money. He needs to part with some of it."

"I don't understand why he would offer to settle, and then send out a hit man."

"Of course, we don't know for sure that it was his hit man. If it was, perhaps they intended to scare, not kill. The guy is either a poor marksman or missed intentionally."

"Then what is the next step?" Cox asked.

"We'll have to see what kind of settlement he will make, and go from there, if you are willing to settle out of court. What do you think would be a fair settlement, Mr. Cox?"

"One thing is for certain. If he did send a hit man, the price just went up!" Cox replied. "You're the attorney. How much do you think I should expect?"

"Quite honestly, I don't think a million dollars is asking enough. We will just have to see how it goes. We want to get you as much as we can, of course."

"Wow! I hadn't even thought of such a huge sum. It's hard to imagine!"

"Then I assume you want to pursue this course?"

"Yes, go for it!"

After leaving the sheriff, Cox drove to the telephone office and made the deposit for a telephone to be installed at his house. It would be done sometime that same day they said. Feeling satisfied, he took the dog home.

The detectives working on the investigation were relentless. They checked through newspapers, police records, courthouse records, questioned neighbors and acquaintances of the Blumfield family, and traced the gunman's rifle back to the seller to learn the buyer's name. On and on it went, Day after day, week after week, while Cox waited.

In the meantime, life for Marlin had become a happy routine. School was out now and the two Goodwin children were enjoying the summer at home. They had learned to accept Marlin as part of the family and liked having him around.

Every day he went with Charles to check the cattle and do what ever chores needed to be done. He mowed the grass, hoed weeds in Mrs. Goodwin's garden and had plenty of fun time with the other kids. They went swimming in the creek, caught crawdads, went frog giging, and climbed trees. It was the best summer Marlin had enjoyed for several years. Cox came over often and went fishing with the kids. They had all grown fond of him as well as his dog.

Cox was always cautious, especially at home. He watched for any strange vehicle coming around and had his ears tuned to any unfamiliar sound. Shep was worth his weight in gold. Nothing escaped his ears or eyes. He loved Cox and would gladly give his life for him. The feeling was mutual.

Week by week, he went over to the Strong place to work on whatever Mrs. Strong needed done. She made sure she had something for him to do, as she enjoyed his company and appreciated his help. Little by little, they reached the point of feeling affection toward one another. Cox was hesitant to ask her out, as it had been so long since he had been in the company of a lady, but eventually he did invite her to see a movie with him. She readily agreed. Privately, she was as thrilled as a high school girl planning her first date!

Cox worked hard cleaning the truck to make it as fit as possible for the date. He washed and buffed the outside, cleaned the inside thoroughly, and worked under the hood, checking fan belts, the oil, etc. He didn't want anything to go wrong on this special occasion. Needless to say, he was excited.

As he was leaning over the fender with his head under the hood, Shep barked. Cox looked up quickly to see the sheriff's car rolling in.

"Wow! What's the occasion? Have you got a date or something?" He ran his hand over the shiny hood of the old truck. "It looks great!" He said approvingly. "Oh, I see you even polished the inside as well. Come on, Cox. What's up?"

"You know, Sheriff, I should tell you it's none of your business, but since you are such a good friend, I'll tell you. I do have a date."

"Ahhh! Let me guess. Could it be the pretty widow Strong? Congratulations!"

"Please, you won't spread it around, will you? I've been out of the loop for so long I am embarrassed. I want to show her a good time, but I am short of confidence."

"I'll keep my mouth shut. You'll do just fine. She's just everyday folk. She won't be expecting caviar and the opera."

"Thanks! Now I know you didn't drive all the way out here to admire my old truck. Do you have something new on the case?"

"Yes I do! Attorney Wilkins called me this morning to tell me that they have gotten Blumfield up to three quarters of a million bucks, and they are still pushing for more. The detectives are onto something with this guy who calls himself Kent Worthington, too. That is not his name. He isn't a professional criminal, but an unemployed man, down on his luck. It looks like he took the job out of desperation. He still won't say who he was working for, but he's weakening. He'll be ready to confess everything by the time he spends another few days in jail. He isn't used to being caged. It really bothers him. You can understand that, I'm sure."

"Very well!"

If he admits it was Blumfield, it will give us more leverage. Blumfield will know he could be facing even more serious charge. If you agree to drop the charges on that and settle the lawsuit out of court, it could go up to the million mark."

"I can't begin to comprehend what it would be like to have that kind of money. What about this Kent? What will happen to him?"

"It all depends on the charges. If he was really trying to kill you or someone else, it will be serious, but if he was just trying to scare you, it could be reduced to a minor offence. I'm sure he will have learned a valuable lesson, either way."

================

The sheriff left and Cox prepared himself for the evening. He had bought himself a new shirt for the occasion, and was spruced up the best he could be, under the circumstances. Someday, he told himself, I will own a three piece suit, with a tie, new dress shoes and a neat little hankie in my breast pocket. Won't that be a sight for sore eyes?

At Mrs. Strong's door, he smoothed his white hair with his hand and waited for her to answer. She came smiling, and looking radiant, Cox thought. Soon they were bouncing along the rough country road toward Allentown, where they had nice places to eat and several theatres.

Driving along, they discussed where to eat and what show they would like to see. Mrs Strong had clipped some ads from the newspaper for names and addresses. They seemed to agree on the kind of food they liked as well as entertainment. They both had simple tastes.

Cox pulled into the parking lot below the sign reading "Country Cooking." They went in and found a booth away from the open window. He was still being cautious, although he had not mentioned the frightening experience of the previous evening to his friend. After the meal, they left for a movie theatre up the street. The movie was starring John Wayne, so they knew they would like it.

Sitting next to her, their shoulders touched. Cox was so happy it was hard to concentrate. He wanted to put his arm across her shoulders, but was afraid of giving the wrong impression. He did finally reach for her hand. She flashed him a warm smile as she laced her fingers into his. This was the best thing that had happened to him for many long years!

When they reached her home, he hurried to open the pickup door and offered his hand, then walked her up the walk and to the door. He felt like a young boy again! He wanted to grab her and hug and kiss her the way he remembered doing when he took his girl to the senior prom, but he wasn't a kid now. He was more interested in winning this good woman's respect at this point, so he would maintain self control. He would be a gentleman. One day, maybe, he would ask permission to kiss her.

They stood at the door, her hands clasped in his, not wanting the evening to end. Finally, he said, "It's been an enjoyable evening. Would you like to do this again sometime?"

"I'd love to, Cox," she replied.

"Then I'll call you. I do have a phone now. Are you in the book?"

"Yes. I'll be waiting to hear from you."

"Good-night then."

"Good-night!"

Cox waited until she had entered the house and closed the door, before bouncing down the steps. He felt like he could jump into the air and click his heels together. What an evening! What a woman! He thought.

He tossed and turned on his cot all night. He was so "cranked up" he could hardly sleep. Shep was restless as well, trying to understand his master's strange new mood.

THE CONFESSION

Rrrrrrrrrrrrrrring! Rrrrrrrrrrrrrrrrring! Rrrrrrrrrrrrrrrrrring! Cox sat up with a start. This was something new to him, to have a telephone ringing in his house and it was unnerving. He rushed to answer it.

"Hello. Cox speaking."

"He did? When?"

"Okay. What time?"

"Thanks Sheriff. I'll be there. Good-bye."

Cox sat down at the table and took a deep breath. He stroked his short beard thoughtfully saying aloud, "I wonder if this means an end to the waiting, or just a lull in the process?"

He went to the box under his cot and brought out a pair of clean sox. He was sure getting tired of carrying water into the house and washing his clothes in a bucket, then hanging them on the barbwire fence to dry. He began to daydream of having a nice house with running water, a washer and dryer and maybe a king sized bed to sleep in.

He dressed and poured Shep some dog food. They both ate, and then left to check the cattle. He didn't waste any time. He had to be in Buckley at 10:00 o'clock to meet the sheriff. He hoped Sheriff Baker wouldn't kid him about his date with Gloria. It was just too precious to share with anyone yet.

The sheriff was waiting at the door and stepped out to meet Cox. They took the sheriff's car to the attorney's office. Sheriff Baker was carrying the paper in his breast pocket. He seemed to be excited about what had been accomplished but didn't offer Cox any explanation, preferring to wait until everyone was present.

The entire group of attorneys was waiting as well as the two detectives who had been working on the case. As soon as they were seated and the door closed, Sheriff Baker began to explain:

"As all of you know, we have been waiting patiently for the suspect we knew as "Kent Worthington" to come clean and tell us what his name really is and what he was doing for whom. Our patience was rewarded yesterday. He called for a pen and paper and confessed the whole thing."

Unfolding the paper, he held it up for all to see. It had bold handwriting on back and front, with a signature at the bottom. Looking at Cox he said "This little piece of paper is worth a lot of money to you, Cox. It will enable us to put the squeeze on Mr. Blumfield and bring this lawsuit to a good conclusion, I hope. Attorney Wilkins, do you want to continue with your information?"

The meeting went on for over an hour, as one after another the men added new information and advice. The detectives told what they had and had not been able to put together. For the most part, it seemed to be very promising. Still, Cox wouldn't allow himself too much hope. He couldn't forget how the legal system failed him before. He sure wasn't going to go out and start buying land on credit with the idea of getting a settlement out of this. If he had learned anything while in prison, it was to wait.

The confession stated that he had been hired by Mr. Blumfield to try to scare Mr. Cox into forgetting about the lawsuit. He had been paid ten thousand dollars up front and promised another twenty thousand when the lawsuit was dropped. His name was actually Fred Peters. He also added a sincere apology to Mr. Cox, Sheriff Baker and anyone else who had suffered as a result of his wrong decision and evil action. He had been unemployed for six months, was about to lose his little ranch, and was behind in all his bills. He acted in desperation. He was very, very sorry.

Attorney Hatfield added, "I know you are thinking the same thing I thought at first. It makes a good story. But I'm inclined to believe he is honestly sorry. He has a family at home and everything was about to fall apart for him. Of course, this didn't fix it, as he'd hoped. He's in even more serious trouble now."

It was Detective Jones' turn to speak. "We learned from his neighbors and friends that he was desperate for a job and couldn't find one. His creditors were hounding him, his wife was about to divorce him and they were foreclosing on his little place. That's about as bad as it gets, but he made the wrong choice."

"How did he get mixed up with Blumfield?" The sheriff asked.

"Blumfield lives a few miles to the north of him and heard about all the trouble. Then Kent or Fred, which ever you want to call him, went to Blumfield to see if he needed a hand around the place. Blumfield saw this as an opportunity and made him an offer he felt he couldn't refuse."

"Did his wife leave him?" Cox asked.

"She's still on the place now, but with him in jail, she is pretty apt to skip out, especially since she has no money for the mortgage or to try to bail him out."

"I can't help feeling sorry for the guy, even though he did scare the fire out of me. I don't want anybody to be locked up unjustly." Cox added.

"Remember, he isn't completely innocent, Cox. He could have killed somebody that night. There are several charges against him."

"I know that. It's just that I keep remembering...."

"Getting back to the lawsuit, Wilkins interjected; the next step is to let Blumfield know that we have this confession and see if we can get the settlement we want. The detectives will drive up that way today. We should know by this time tomorrow what he has to say. It won't take long to draw up the necessary documents."

Cox was silent as he drove home. He didn't even talk to Shep about it. He still ha doubts about the outcome. Something about this whole thing just didn't smell right.

He couldn't really put his finger on the problem, but he was troubled. His hopes and dreams were dependent on it all working out in his favor, but after his past experience, he was suspicious. An uneasy feeling crept into his mind. He desperately *needed* to have it succeed.

He was supposed to go over to the Goodwin's place in the afternoon. They had realized that Marlin had had a birthday on the last day of May and they had missed it, so they were having a party for him today. Cox had shopped for a gift for him but it was not an easy thing to do. He was at a loss to know what to get for the kid. He had very little spare money either, so he called Mrs. Strong about it.

"I'm so glad you called, Cox," she said. "I have been invited to the party as well and I have already bought him a cowboy hat and a pair of leather gloves. If you want to, I'll just put your name on it with mine. That will take care of it, don't you think?"

"That's a great idea, but you'll have to let me pay half..."

"Now, don't worry. We'll work that out."

"I guess I'll see you at the party then."

"Yes. I'm looking forward to it."

The birthday party was a joyful occasion. Marlin was overjoyed with the gifts. He wore the hat all afternoon as he ran and played games with the other youngsters. He almost made a nuisance of himself trying to show his gratitude for the gifts. He had received numerous things from the Goodwins, as well as the other guests. He thought this was the happiest time he had had for several years.

Mr. and Mrs. Goodwin, Mrs. Strong and Cox sat in the shade of the trees enjoying the children at play. Suddenly Charles asked, "Cox, what's the latest on the lawsuit?"

Gloria glanced at Cox in surprise. Cox said slowly, "I haven't yet shared with Gloria that part of my life, Charles. She doesn't know what you are talking about."

"Oh, I'm sorry, Cox. I assumed she knew the whole story."

"No, but she is about to hear it now" Cox said with a smile.

"Now, Cox, if you'd rather not......" Gloria responded.

"I've been looking for an opportunity to tell you about it. Now seems to be the perfect time. Have you told you wife about it, Charles?"

"I have told her some of it but I'm sure she would like to hear it from you. That way she'll be sure to get it straight."

So Cox began with the day he rode away from his parents' ranch, with such optimism, and hope, and continued all the way through to the day they all met. They listened with great interest and empathy until he had concluded.

"I have to hand it to you Cox. Most people would be bitter and vengeful, but you seem to be so congenial. I really admire your attitude." Mrs. Goodwin said.

"I am speechless!" Mrs. Strong said. "I never would have imagined you had suffered through so much. How long has it been since you were set free?"

"It's been about a year now. It's always fresh in my mind. It's hard to put away."

"I'm sure it would be."

"What about the lawsuit? What is happening with that?" Charles wanted to know.

"I'm glad you ask about that because I was hoping to get a chance to ask your opinion about it. We had a meeting with all the people who are helping with it just this morning. You would think I would be excited about it, but I'm not. For some reason I feel that there is something wrong with the whole picture. I don't know what it could be, or why I feel that way all of a sudden, but it's like a dark cloud of doom lurking over my head. I have studied it until I am blue in the face but I can't figure out the problem. I hope you can help me."

They were all quiet for awhile, and then Mrs. Strong spoke. "We are all Christians here, are we not? I think this might be a spiritual problem. I suggest we bow before the Lord and ask His help with this. He certainly knows what's going on."

Everyone agreed and they joined hands and each one prayed, asking for wisdom and guidance from on high. They asked for God's peace and assurance to guide Cox through the legal process ahead of him.

It was a blessed time. Cox felt a great burden lift from his shoulders. No one had prayed for him like that since he was a kid, at home with his parents. He was refreshed and encouraged.

The kids came rushing from the back yard and crowded into the little gathering. Marlin sat next to Cox on the picnic bench. He had his arm around Cox's shoulders every chance he got. He felt a strange, deep bond with him. Cox was more than pleased to have him near. He sincerely loved the boy.

The party was over and everyone began to leave. Cox walked Mrs. Strong to her car. She paused a moment, then asked if he would be interested in attending church with her the following Sunday. He agreed to go. He hadn't been in a church for many years. It was something he longed to do.

They decided to go in her car this time. He left for home feeling that he had had a good, worthwhile day after all.

Shep heard all about it on the trip home. He was a good listener. He interrupted only one time and that was to lick Cox's hand.

Cox puttered around his place, he began to allow himself to dream. The dark cloud of worry about the legal proceedings disappeared, and in its place a glimmer of hope was rising. He became aware of the leading of the Lord now. He had never really experienced this before. It was a wonderful feeling.

"Shep, let's go for a drive," he said. Shep bounded toward the pickup with his tail wagging excitedly. They slowly rumbled along the graveled roads, studying the fields, pastures and fences. Eventually, they came to the Kester place, where Marlin had been taken a month earlier. Just the sight of the dreary place made Cox shudder as he recalled what could have happened to the boy that day. Yet he had become fascinated with the possibilities he invisioned here.

As he and Shep made their way through the underbrush and weeds, they discovered the remains of livestock pens, the foundation of an old barn, a cistern and a windmill that had fallen to the ground.

"It would sure take a lot of work to put this place back into shape, Shep. I don't know whether I'm up to the challenge or not. I like the location though. I think I'll check into it further. I don't even know if it's for sale."

Cox drove around the section, studying the terrain. He soon arrived at the Goodwin place. Charles was near the barn and met him at the drive way.

"Hello there. I didn't expect to see you again so soon. What's up?"

Cox stepped out of his vehicle and greeted Charles warmly. "After our prayer together yesterday, the dark cloud lifted and I began to dream again. I was out looking around to see if there might be some land for sale that would be suitable for the ranch I want to build for kids. I ended up over at the Kester place. You know, that place has a lot of possibilities. Do you happen to know why it is just setting there going to waste?"

"They say the folks died and left no heirs. They didn't have a will so it wasn't designated to anyone. That's just talk, of course. I never had any occasion to check it out. You could go to a real estate agent. If they didn't know, they would find out. You know how it is if there's a chance to make a commission."

"Yes, that's right, I guess. The sheriff might be able to give me some information about it as well. Thanks for your help. I think I'll drive into Bucklin again."

Charles stood and watched Cox drive away. He didn't quite know what to make of the guy, but he did have a lot of respect for him. He hoped everything would work out well.

Marlin came from the barn just as Cox drove off.

"Was that Cox," he asked.

"Yes, it was. He has big things crowding his mind today."

"I guess that's why he didn't look for me," Marlin said disappointedly.

"Don't take it personally, Marlin. He'll be back."

Just as they turned back to their chores, Cox did return. He stepped out of pickup quickly as Marlin ran to meet him. They embraced as Cox said "I don't know what was wrong with me Marlin. I was really preoccupied. I'm sorry!"

"But you did come back. Thanks, Cox."

He was on the road to Bucklin within a few minutes, satisfied that he had not completely ruined Marlin's opinion of him. Being a second "dad" was great, but it did require some commitment. He would work on that.

He drove directly to the sheriff's office. Baker was out on business for the county and would be gone most of the day. He left and drove around the little town. On a whim, he drove out two miles looking for Marlin's former home. He knew about where it was located and from Marlin's description he recognized the place at once. It was a neat little cottage type structure, with a picket fence across the front. He saw what used to be flower beds here and there and pens in the rear for livestock. There were no chickens, horse or cow that he could see anyway. He had to wonder whether Bert had sold them after his late wife passed away. "He's a sorry jerk!" Cox said aloud.

Shep whined and licked his face, sensing his anger. They drove to the next junction and whipped a U and came back by. A car was pulling into the driveway. Cox slowed down to get a look at the guy. Burt got out and stumbled toward the house gripping the neck of a liquor bottle. Cox went on down the road to Bucklin and parked in front of a building bearing a sign which read "Bucklin Real Estate."

He was invited to take a chair across the desk from the realtor. After stating his business, the man began to go through the file cabinet until he found a thick file of papers. He placed them on his desk and rifled through them looking for just the right one. Finally, he stopped to read awhile, then looking up he said, "It looks like the place was abandoned in 1980 when Mrs. Kester passed away. Her husband had died two years earlier. They had no children. There was no will."

A moment later he said "The state is about due to sell it for taxes. I could go to the courthouse and check it out, if you want. The taxes could get pretty high as there are estate taxes, the cost of probate, etc. I can't tell you for sure what all might be included until I research it."

"I'm probably "jumping the gun'" by even asking at this point. Just hold off until I get some things settled. I'm not ready to make any commitment on it right away." Cox rose to his feet saying, "I'll get back to you on it later. Thanks."

===============

"I must be nuts to think this is going to work out. It would take a lot of money to build the necessary living quarters, barns and corrals, besides hiring the help, buying livestock, etc. The dream seemed to be outgrowing his ability. Would he be able to do it? He would certainly need some advice and help from others because he didn't know how to begin, what the law requires or any of that.

"Maybe I should just forget the whole idea," he told Shep. It was time to do his chores and take a walk. He had a lot of thinking to do.

71

All the information, the plans, the misgivings, the hopes and dreams kept running through his mind like cars on the track at the Indy 500. Some spinning out of control, some hitting the wall, some crashing and burning, but always there remained a few to finish the course. There has to be a winner. But right now, his mind needed to make a pit stop. It was more than he could deal with alone. It takes a large crew to keep a race car on the track and it was going to take a crew to keep Cox's dream going as well. Right now, he just needed to pull back and rethink the whole thing.

Cox was scheduled to work for Gloria Strong again the next day, so he drove to her place early hoping to get a lot of work done and have time to spend with her, as well. He had promised to call and set a time for another get-together, but he would ask her in person. When he arrived, her lights were on. She came out to greet him and explain the work she needed done that day. She planned to have a little vegetable garden, so she wanted that worked, while she mowed the grass. It was a beautiful morning to be out in the fresh air doing meaningful things, especially with someone around who mattered, and Cox mattered.

By mid-morning they had finished with those chores and she invited him to take a break and drink some tea. They sat on the patio enjoying the coffee cake and tea and one another. They discussed their week-end date and set the time and place. He would wait until then to ask her advice about the ranch for boys. Soon the day had ended and he made his way back home. It became harder and harder to tear himself away from this special woman.

MARLIN'S BOOTS

Time seemed to drag as he waited for some new development in the lawsuit. He was thankful for the friendships he enjoyed now with he Blacks, the Goodwins, Sheriff Baker and especially, Mrs. Strong. He made it a point to see Marlin every couple of days, at least. He seemed to always be wearing the cowboy hat Gloria had given him. Charles was teaching the boy horsemanship, and he took to it like a duck to water. Cox thought he needed a pair of boots, but he just didn't have the money to buy them for him right now.

He leaned against the rail fence watching the two as they worked to train a young foal to lead. It was incredible how quickly the colt learned to move forward, away from the butt rope and was soon responding to the slightest tug on the lead rope snapped to the halter. Charles was so patient and encouraging to both youngsters.

Shep barked, warning Cox of an approaching vehicle. It was Jim Black arriving. He walked to the corral fence, carrying a bulging paper bag. He watched the training session with interest.

"The boy sure likes that hat, doesn't he?'

"He does. He's wearing it every time I see him since the party."

"I'm sorry we missed the party. They had asked us to come, but we had a previous commitment."

"You did send gifts though. I appreciate that. I know he's not my boy, but I sort of feel like he is."

"I got to thinking about him riding horses out here, and my son had three pairs of boots in the closet. We decided to give Marlin a pair of them, if they will fit. They are nearly new. He got them about a month before the accident." A pained expression covered his face as he mentioned that sad day.

"I'm sorry you had to go through such a loss. I know Marlin will be excited about the boots. I never did tell him about you son. Charles may have, since they have become so close. They have a lot of time together to talk about all kinds of things. It's been good for the kid. Every kid needs a good father and he's never had one before."

The training session was over and they returned the foal to the pen where his anxious mother was waiting. He ran to her and began to nurse. His little audience all chuckled with satisfaction. This was a group of horse lovers for sure.

Marlin rushed to greet Cox and Jim Black, carrying the lead rope in his hand. Cox thought of his own early days on the ranch, learning the art of horsemanship. He was glad Marlin had this opportunity to do the same.

Jim apologized for not being able to come to the birthday party, and then handed the bag to Marlin saying, "I brought you these boots. I hope they will fit. They belonged to Dakota."

Marlin took the bag and peeked inside. A wide smile crossed his face as he threw his arms around Jim's neck. Tears filled Jim's eyes. They had both suffered the loss of one so near and dear to them and no words were necessary.

Marlin sat on an overturned feed bucket and began to remove his old worn tennis shoes and pull on the boots. "They are just right." he exclaimed and began to walk back and forth, looking at the boots, then at the men. "They feel great!" Everyone chuckled at the great joy expressed in the boy's face.

"Thank you so much!" he said. "Thank you so much! This is awesome!"

"You are entirely welcome, Marlin. I know you will make good use of them. That makes me happy."

"I can't wait to go riding again and see how much difference they make. Do you think the horse will notice?"

"If you put some spurs on I guarantee he will notice." Cox replied with a smile.

The men thoroughly enjoyed the hopping and jumping of the excited boy. He was *so* happy! He knew he was in the proper attire for life on a ranch and he was ready for it.

As Mr. Black left, Marlin rushed to the house to show off his new boots to Mrs. Goodwin and the kids. Cox and Charles walked slowly toward Cox's truck.

"You must have told Marlin about the death of Jim's son Dakota?"

"Yes. The kids had told him some of the details so he wanted to know more about it. I hated to tell him, but I guess he would find out sooner or later. I figured it would upset him more since he lost his mother at about the same time. A ranch is the best place in the world for a kid to grow up, but things do happen. It can be dangerous."

"I don't think I ever heard exactly what did happen to the boy."

"I understand that they were out sorting some cattle in the corral. Dakota was handling the gate when a big cow went crazy and charged him. It was such a surprise to them as she had never acted that way before. She hit him in the chest with her head and pinned him to the gate post. His chest was crushed and he died instantly. It was really hard on the family. He was real special to them, being the only boy. He was a lot of help to Jim, too. They worked together at everything. He was quite a cowboy too. He could ride broncos, rope calves, and even did some bull dogging. He loved rodeo."

"I can tell he still grieves for the boy. He probably blames himself for it. So many parents do, even though there was nothing he could have done to prevent it. To have it happen right there before his eyes made it even harder, I'm sure."

"Yes, they say he grabbed him up and ran to the pickup with him and drove like a mad man to the hospital. His wife didn't know anything about it until he called to tell her their son was dead. They are both strong believers in the Lord, though. Their faith in Him is what got them through it."

"I can't think of anything worse than to lose a child. By the way, Charles, have you ever looked at the Kester place closely?"

"No, I've never had a reason to."

"If you have a little time, I'd like to take you over there to see it."

"Yeah, let's go. What have you found out about it?"

Riding along, they discussed the legalities, pro and con. Then they walked through the house and around the grounds trying to evaluate what it might be worth. Charles agreed that it would be a challenge and take a lot of "sweat equity " to put it back into shape, but if it could be bought reasonably enough, it would be worth it.

As they returned, Mrs. Goodwin came to the door and yelled to them to come in for lunch. She had prepared for Cox as well.

They were just sitting down when the sheriff came wheeling into the drive. He rushed to the door and spoke to Cox. "I have something important to tell you," he said motioning for him to come outside. "I didn't want to talk in front of the family. We have a problem."

The door closed and Sheriff Baker continued. "I'm not sure what this is going to do to the case, but Blumfield was found dead in his home yesterday."

"What!" Cox exclaimed. "How? What happened?"

"It's still under investigation, of course, but they are calling it a suicide."

Cox groaned. "I don't know what to say. I can't honestly say that I'm sorry after what he did to me, but I wouldn't wish for this either. I wonder what effect it will have on my case against him."

"There is no way to know at this point, although he did sign the papers before he died, agreeing to a million dollar settlement. They found it on his desk. Even that doesn't give me any assurance that it's a done deal, because there are so many questions being asked."

"What kind of questions?"

"The usual kind; did he sign it under duress? Could someone have forced him to sign it, and then kill him?"

Panic suddenly crossed Cox's face. "You don't suppose they think *I* did it, do you?"

"I didn't want to worry you, Cox, but they will very likely want to question you."

Cox covered his face with his hands. "Oh dear Lord! Not again," he groaned.

"I don't think you have anything to worry about, Cox. You have a good alibi, I'm sure, and witnesses as to where you were when it happened."

"I had a good alibi forty years ago too, but you know what good that did!" He was visibly shaken, fearful and angry. He wanted to run, but how, and where? He knew he couldn't hide. The "fight or flight" instinct engulfed him, sweeping away all the peace that had come to him over the past year. His self control was almost overwhelmed. He began to tremble violently.

The sheriff put his arm around Cox's shoulders and guided him to the picnic table where he could sit down. He took several deep breaths, trying to calm his nerves. He was in a real dilemma. All the mistrust of the legal system was pounding on his door again. The fear of being falsely accused of a crime and thrown into prison for a second time seemed a very strong possibility. He was temped to blame the sheriff for this problem, since he had persuaded him to file the lawsuit in the first place.

The sheriff continued to reassure him that all would be well. He must believe that.

"I won't abandon you, Cox," he said. "I'm going to be here for you. I'll do everything in my power to see that you are not misjudged again, believe me."

Charles joined them, curious to know what was going on. The sheriff briefed him on the situation. He was very concerned about Cox, as he could see the anxiety in his face.

His two friends urged Cox to come into the house and eat something, or at least have a cup of coffee. He relented and they entered the house together. Charles poured him some coffee, and then asked if he would like to have his plate of food warmed. He tried to show some interest in the good meal Diane had prepared, but he had lost his appetite.

The men sat at the table and tried to come up with a plan as to what could be done. Sheriff Baker thought it would be better for Cox to stay with the Goodwins until they could talk to a lawyer, at least. He didn't need to be alone and vulnerable.

It was agreed that he would remain with Charles while Sheriff Baker made a trip to Bucklin to talk to the attorneys group.

"Cox, I need to go check some cattle out in the northeast corner of the east pasture. I'll have to ride a horse to get to them, as its rough terrain. If you'd like to ride along, I've got another horse out there."

"That sounds like a good distraction. I haven't been on a horse in years, but as you know, it's not something you forget how to do. I'll do it. Joking, he asked, "Do you suppose I could wear Marlin's boots?"

"Hey, I've got extra boots. What size do you wear?"

"Eight and a half, I think. I haven't bought boots for awhile."

Charles returned with a pair. "These are nines. I'll bet they will work."

In a short while the two were riding across the prairie, side by side. It was good therapy for Cox. He felt right at home in the saddle again. The sun was warm, the air fragrant from tree blossoms. The jingle of the bit chain, the squeak of leather and the steady clopping of the horses hooves helped settle his frayed nerves. It felt *so* good to be astride a horse again.

As they unsaddled the horses, Sheriff Baker returned. He had had a fruitful session with the attorneys and could hardly wait to tell Cox. In spite of all the complications, it looked like everything would work out well after all. It was too early to say for certain, but the initial investigation seemed to indicate that Blumfield did committ suicide after signing the papers the detectives had left with him the day before. His wife had fretted herself to an early grave over her son's wayward life and later, her husband's crooked dealings to cover the murder. Being a devout Christian, she couldn't deal with such treachery. His only son was dead and Mr. Blumfield was all alone with his money, which had brought him nothing but trouble, anyway. He had written a letter to his attorney and mailed it before putting the gun into his mouth and pulling the trigger. He had explained the whole story to him, confessed to bribing the judge, the jurors, the prison wardens, a number of lawyers and even the mail clerks at the prison, to keep the truth from being known about Cox. Finally he had confessed to hiring Fred Perkins to shoot at Cox. It had all been for nothing; and now he was glad to give Cox all the money he had left. There was no one else to give it to anyway. He signed off with,

"Born to lose,"

Rusty Blumfield

As they all drew together, reading a copy of the letter from Blumfield, there was a long silence. Finally Charles spoke:

"This is incredible" he said. Two hours ago old Cox was practically looking down the barrel of a gun, and now he's a millionaire! "They all laughed as the other two pounded Cox on the back, congratulating him.

"What a way to end the day," Cox said. "I doubt if I will be able to sleep tonight. At first I was expecting to be handcuffed and now I'll be worried about being robbed of all that money!"

They were a much more cheerful trio when they parted that evening.

Things seemed to settle into a calm routine as Cox waited for the attorneys to get all the paper work done. As is always the case, there was a mountain of it to be worked through to satisfy the legal system. There was no way to rush it though. There were searches, subpoenas, investigations of witnesses, court hearings, etc.; the list goes on and on. But Cox was continually assured by them that it was just a matter of time. How much time, they couldn't tell. So he kept busy. He looked at properties, researched the legal aspects of running a boys ranch; he checked on insurance, talked to prospective board members, house parents, cooks and housekeepers. He spent long hours at the table figuring the cost of livestock for the boys, as well as farming equipment, clothing, and food. He was beginning to think there was no end of things to consider. Would he have enough money to do this? One million dollars seemed to be very inadequate when he put it all on paper.

Once more, he found himself going to Charles Goodwin for advice. Marlin came running, wearing the boots, the hat and a big smile. It pleased Cox beyond measure to see this boy so happy. Why wouldn't he want to help other kids as well?

In the shade of the oak tree, the two men discussed the prospect of the ranch for boys. "You are planning an organization that is way beyond a million dollars, Cox. What you are forgetting is that there is government help for most of these troubled youngsters, which follows them. Churches and individuals will help with it. You won't have to be responsible for the funding. Your most important contribution will be the heart to do it. There are very few people who would even dream of such a commitment."

"I'm beginning to have second thoughts about it, myself."

"I can certainly understand that. This is huge. After you get it all down on paper as to what you want to do, you'll probably need to have a meeting with all the people interested in helping with it. You'll need the board members, lawyers, contributors and government reps. You should have an estimate of the cost of the overall project, as well as the day to day expenses first. At least that's my thoughts on it."

"That does sound like the logical way to start. I hadn't considered that there would be other financing available. I guess I wasn't reading the right kind of stuff when I was in prison all those years. If I had known all this would happen, I could have gotten myself a good education. Then I'd know what to do. As they say, "hindsight is always 20-20.""

His loyal companion, Shep, say quietly at his feet waiting. They were almost inseparable. Cox would be completely lost without him now. True to his work, Sheriff Baker faithfully checked with him concerning the dog food supply. It was rewarding to him to see the strong bond between the two.

Cox had a lot of thinking to do. He needed to decide whether this endeavor was something he was capable of handling. He decided he would need a good C.E.O., who had the knowledge, the education and the wisdom to put it all together and run the place. But how would he find such a person? He came face to face with the reality that only God knew. But he knew God!

At home again, he made it a matter of prayer. Every time he began to feel overwhelmed by it, he would pray. He was trying to learn just what it meant to "cast your burdens on the Lord."

Cox had managed to pinch enough pennies out of his earnings from working for Gloria to buy himself a nice pair of blue jeans for their week-end dates. He was freshly shaven, had a new hair cut and wore his new outfit when he knocked at her door this time.

"Oh! Look at you!" she exclaimed upon opening the door. "My, you do look handsome! Come in and sit a spell. I'm almost ready."

She disappeared into the hallway while Cox sat at her table admiring how neat everything looked. She was a good housekeeper, and knew how to decorate. It was tasteful, but not extravagant.

She returned to the kitchen with a necklace in her hand. "Would you mind fastening this for me?" She asked.

"You'll have to show me the combination. I've never done this sort of thing before."

"Okay. Just pull this little sliding thing back, and then hook it into the other ring and let go. It's easy enough." She turned her back to him, allowing him to drop it over her head and work the clasp. He was slightly "twitter patted" being so close to her. He allowed his hands to rest on her shoulders momentarily. She reached up and took hold of them, then releasing her hold, turned to face him. They stood close together for a few seconds while cupid worked his magic. Suddenly they were embracing one another tightly, their hearts beating hard and fast. Cox could hardly breathe. This was wonderful beyond words! He didn't want to ever let her go! But wisdom prevailed. Whether Cox knew it or not, Gloria knew that this could lead to more serious emotional consequences, that they were neither one ready for.

"We'd better get going. We don't want to be late" she said, blushing. Soon they were on the way to Allentown again. He looked forward to a tasty meal, a good movie, and the company of an exciting woman. What a great way to spend an evening!

GOODWIN'S SURPRISE

It was late June. Flower blossoms brightened the homesteads, the road ditches and the prairie. The gardens were producing radishes, leaf lettuce, and spinach, while the beans, peas, tomatoes, okra, squash, and all the melons were racing to see which would mature first. It was a very busy time out on the Goodwin ranch.

Charles and Marlin were always talking about the new calves. It was a relief to have all of them out on pasture with their mothers. The prairie hay was ready to be cut and baled. Then it would have to be hauled in out of the field and stacked in the barn. The big round bales would be lined up along the fence row. Marlin was a lot of help to Charles. He was growing larger and stronger every day from all the exercise, and he enjoyed it. This was the kind of life he had dreamed about. It was a useful, satisfying life.

Diane and the younger children kept busy with the garden and yard. Kendra was learning to cook and help her mother with the housework. Mark kept the grass cut and hoed the garden.

Cox came every day or two and helped with what ever was being done at the moment. It gave him great joy to be able to work the cattle or help in the garden or yard. He was fond of all the family. He was diligently working on the plans for the ranch for boys... People had heard about it and some had offered to help any way they could. This was a big encouragement to Cox, knowing that they had likely heard also that he was an ex-con. He was guiltless, but an ex-con, nonetheless.

Mid-July was unbearably hot and humid. Mrs. Goodwin made it a point to go out early to pick the garden while it was cool. She was picking the beans one morning when she began to feel dizzy. Thinking it was from all the bending over, she straightened up and took several deep breaths of air. Her head was spinning! She called to Mark, who was mowing nearby. He couldn't hear above the noise of the lawn mower and kept going. Suddenly she collapsed to the ground, spilling the pail of beans in the dirt. Several minutes passed before Mark noticed her lying there. He cut the engine and ran to her yelling, "Mother! Mother!" Kneeling beside her, he patted her face and begged her to speak to him, but she was out cold.

He ran to the house calling to his sister. "Kendra! Come quick! Something has happened to Mother. She's lying on the ground in the garden! Here, take this wet towel and wash her face. I'm going after Dad!"

Kendra ran to the garden and fell to her knees beside her mother. She began wiping her face and calling to her, but there was no response. She became more frightened every second. She began to sob hysterically. She had never had to deal with anything like this before. She thought her mother might be dead.

Mark ran to the hay field so fast he was out of breath and could hardly make himself understood. Charles quickly unhitched the mowing machine and drove the tractor home and across the yard to the garden. He rushed to his wife's side calling to her just as his children had done. When she didn't respond, he ran to get the car. He scooped her up and placed her on the back seat, as he yelled instructions to the kids. Spinning the wheels, the car raced up the road.

At the hospital, the attendants quickly brought a gurney and wheeled her to the emergency room, where the nurses and emergency room physician began to check her vital signs and administer medication.

Great concern etched Charles' face as he watched the activity. He prayed silently for wisdom for the doctor and for a good outcome for his wife and his family.

Diane's eyes fluttered, and then opened wide with bewilderment.

"Where am I? What is going on?" she asked.

Charles stepped to her side. The nurses reassured her that she was all right.

"You fainted. That's all," they said.

Charles took her hand in his. "How do you feel, honey?" he asked.

"I feel okay. I'm embarrassed. I don't know what's going on. How did I get here?"

"Do you remember fainting out in the garden?"

"Oh, yeah, I do remember. I became real dizzy and then fell. I wonder why that happened."

"I recommend that you go to your primary physician right away and get a good checkup," the doctor interjected. "He will be able to tell you what's going on."

They called their physician and got an appointment for 2:00 o'clock. This gave them time to drive home and let the children know their mother was all right. The three were nearly frantic with concern. They had called Cox, who rushed over to be with them during the wait. Mrs. Goodwin assured them that she was fine. She would know more about what caused her "spell" after the doctor's appointment later in the day.

After a quick lunch, Diane and Charles left again. Cox and Marlin went to the field. As Cox mowed, Shep and Marlin ran along beside the tractor, romping and playing. They chased field mice and kangaroo rats and an occasional cotton tailed rabbit. The warm sunshine and fresh air was stimulating. They were like bucket calves let out of the stall.

Upon their return from the doctor, Charles and Diane were flushed with excitement. The children were confused, as they expected some gloomy medical forecast, but that was not the case. The four members of the family were alone so they had a private moment to share the good news. There was going to be a fifth member to the family!

Kendra was ecstatic. "I hope it's a girl. I hope it's a girl" She danced up and down and whirled around, her long dark hair flying. Mark remained quiet and thoughtful. Finally he asked, "Why did you faint, Mother? Is that normal?"

"No Mark, it isn't normal but it does happen occasionally. They don't really know why. It has never happened to me before and probably won't happen again." She reached over and tousled his hair. "Now, don't you worry about it. I'm just fine."

The tractor roared in behind the barn, so Charles and Mark went to help out. Cox stepped down and hurried to meet them, anxious to know about Diane's condition. "How is Diane? Is she okay?"

"She's just fine, Cox," Charles said with a grin.

"Well then, what *was* wrong?" He looked from one to the other confused.

Mark hung his head shyly. "She's pregnant," he said quietly.

The two men exchanged a wink and a wide grin. Cox gave Charles a "thumbs up" as they turned to service the tractor.

Cox made the ten mile drive south to Bucklin, as was his custom every Monday morning to meet with the men working on the lawsuit. There were usually papers to sign and questions to answer and to ask. It seemed to him that this thing was taking *forever*. The confidence of the attorneys assured him that all was well and it wouldn't take more than a few months to finish.

He left their office feeling a little down. "A few months" sounded like an eternity to him. So much time had been lost from his life unnecessarily and a few more months subtracted from the remaining years he had on the earth just didn't seem fair. Fair? What am I thinking? Is there any guarantee that life is going to be fair? Has it ever been fair to me? Has it been fair to anyone? There is so much injustice in this world, he thought. Oh, okay. There is another life after this one is over. In it, all is life and light, love and beauty. It won't be "fair." The scales will be tipped in our favor. Jesus made sure of that at the cross, he reminded himself.

He saw Sheriff Baker driving along the narrow street and beckoned to him. They parked side by side to talk.

"I'm curious, Sheriff. What did you find out about Marlin's home place? How is it deeded?"

"I was talking to the Registrar of Deeds only yesterday. She told me that Mrs. Simpson had been in her office about a month before she married Mr. Simpson. She asked that her name be replaced on the title deed with Marlin's name. Apparently she had some misgivings about the man she was about to marry and wanted to protect the property.

85

"Do you mean to tell me that the place rightfully belongs to Marlin?"

"That's right."

"Is there any way Bert can get his hands on it? Legally, I mean?"

"That is completely out of my area of expertise, Cox. I don't know."

Cox pondered this new problem as the old pickup rattled along the dusty country road toward home. I guess it's none of my business, but if she wanted her son to have that place, he ought to have it. Bert has no right to it. I wonder if they even know where Marlin is living. If the taxes are his to pay, that could be a problem. Maybe Bert paid them to prevent anyone from contacting Marlin. I wonder....

After lunch he drove to see Gloria Strong. Working for her had been such a blessing. It not only helped him financially, but seeing her lifted his spirits tremendously. Their relationship was growing closer with each passing day. They had gotten past the hand holding stage and on to embracing and even a brief kiss. He was in love with her, but didn't reveal his feelings to her. He wanted to retain self control and was afraid he might not be able to if he expressed his true feelings. Or she might be insulted and slap his face, he thought. He didn't *think* she would, but he wasn't going to risk it.

They greeted one another with a quick embrace at the door. "Come in" she said, pulling a chair out from the table. "Let's chat a bit."

This is interesting, he thought. She must have something on her mind. I hope it's good. She poured tea in two cups, placed creamer and sugar before him, then sat across the table from him.

"I have been thinking about this dream of yours, she said. I have intentionally avoided telling you of my experience as supervisor of a facility similar to what you are contemplating until now. I waited to see how serious you were."

"You ran a youth home?" He was surprised.

"I sure did. I was the "head man" for a number of years. "There is more to me than meets the eye," She laughed.

"This is exciting! Are you willing to help put this thing together, then?"

"Why do you think I told you this? Of course I am."

Cox was elated. He jumped up and took her hands and danced her around the kitchen in delight. "I'm so excited, he exclaimed. "This is really good news. Forgetting his earlier resolutions, he grabbed her in a bear hug and kissed her full on the mouth. "I love you!" He said.

Gloria was completely taken aback. "What did you say?"

"I'm sorry, Gloria. I hadn't meant to tell you. At least not yet, but it's true. I have known for quite some time that I have gone off the deep end. I hope you aren't offended."

"Offended? No! I'm thrilled! I feel the same way about you."

As they stood hand in hand, their eyes glistened with joy from deep inside their hearts. "This is unbelievable. This is wonderful," Cox said over and over. He kissed her again, then dropping to one knee he asked, "Gloria, will you marry me?"

"You don't waste any time, do you, Cox? Yes, I will marry you!"

Cox rose to his feet and took her into his arms again. "Oh, Gloria," he said. This is the happiest day of my entire life. No doubt about it."

After finally tearing himself away from Gloria, he did the repair work she had requested and left for the Goodwin ranch. As usual, Marlin came running, wearing his cowboy hat and boots. Cox was so swept away by his morning with Gloria that he didn't notice the change in Marlin's disposition..

"How is Mrs. Goodwin?"

"She is having some problems. She doesn't seem happy or maybe it's because she's sick. I'm not sure. They don't tell me their family stuff. I'm not real "family," anyway."

Cox, now aware of the change, put his arm around Marlin's shoulders as they walked. "Marlin, what's wrong? Is it that you are concerned about Diane?"

"I am concerned, but things are different around here lately. I feel like an outsider now that there is a baby on the way."

"I don't see how that would make any difference. This family really cares about you, Marlin."

"They used to, but now I'm not so sure. Diane yells at me sometimes and Charles is grumpy. Kendra and Mark just sit in front of the television.

They never want to go play catch or anything. It's just not the same anymore, Cox"

"I'm sorry, Marlin. I'm sure it's only temporary. I'll try to find out what's bothering them. We'll try to work it out, Son." He gave the boy a quick embrace and they entered the house.

It was late august and the weather was sweltering hot. The air conditioner was working overtime to keep the house comfortable for the family. Mrs. Goodwin was stretched out on the couch resting as they entered. She sat up and began to apologize.

"No need to apologize, Diane. You need to take care of yourself. How are you feeling, anyway? Have you had any more fainting spells?"

"No, none at all, although I'm having a difficult pregnancy this time. The Doctor told me to get lots of rest. I may have to stay in bed full time the last three months."

"When is the baby due?"

"Not until February. It seems like a long time from now."

"I'm sure it does. Where is Charles? Out in the hay field?"

"No, he's finished with the hay. He may be out checking on the cattle. Go on out and look if you like. I'm sure you will find him."

He and Marlin went out looking for Charles. They walked across the hay field to look across to the pasture where the cows were contentedly grazing. They could see Charles's hat as he squatted near a calf lying on the ground.

"It looks like he has a sick one, Marlin. Let's go see if we can help him out."

As they approached, the calf tried to get up. "Hi Cox. This calf has been snake bit. He is pretty sick. I need to get him to a vet. Will you bring my pickup out here for me?"

"You've got it," Cox said as he headed back across the hay field. Within minutes, the calf was loaded and they were headed to town. Marlin ran into the house to let Diane know, and then jumped back into the pickup bed to keep the calf calm on the ride.

The ride to the veterinarian afforded Cox an opportunity to explore the difficulty Marlin was having at the ranch.

"How is everything going at the ranch, Charles?" Cox inquired.

"It's going pretty well. Diane is having a lot of difficulty with this pregnancy. She's sick a lot and gets short with the kids, especially Marlin."

"Does he antagonize her somehow?"

"Not that I have seen. He tries too hard, maybe. He seems to think it's his responsibility to keep everyone happy. That can be irritating at times."

"Do you think I should find another place for the boy? I don't want him to cause you a problem, Charles."

"Look Cox. You didn't have anything to do with him being here. He came on his own, and we took him in on our own."

"I know. You're right, but I feel so responsible for him. He came to me first. I need to help him out."

"Things will be better after the baby comes."

"That is several months away. That is a long time for a kid to feel..."

"Unwanted?"

"Unnecessary is the word I was going to use."

The men rode along in silence, each deep in thought. Turning to Cox, Charles said, "I really care for Marlin. He is a great kid. If my boy turns out as well as he, I'll be a very proud father. He has worked like a trooper all summer long. He has never refused to do anything I ask him and never talked back. He doesn't fuss and fight with my kids, eats whatever is set before him, keeps himself clean.... I honestly can't fault him in anything. I don't want to lose him, Cox, but I want him to be happy as well. What do you suggest we do to correct this?"

Cox thought hard for a few moments then said, "I think you need to sit down and talk to him, you and your wife together. Explain how you feel and let him tell you how he feels. That might clear the air and give you a fresh start. What do you think?"

"I think you are onto something, my friend. Give me five!" As they did a high five, relief swept over both men like a cool breeze on a hot summer day. It was almost as if the problem was already solved.

As the veterinarian administered anti-venom medication to the sick calf, the three guys watched with interest and concern. Charles didn't like to have any of his critters suffer, and he certainly didn't want to have the mother cow grieve over her dead calf.

"He'll be all right by tomorrow. They bounce back quickly when you catch it in time. He is breathing easier already."

When they got to the pasture gate, the cow was waiting. She bellowed for her baby and when they opened the gate she rushed to the pickup to sniff him, trying to make sure it was her own... They drove to the barn with her following close behind. They carried the calf inside the barn stall and placed him on the ground. The cow immediately began to lick him, mooing softly. They left them alone to rebuild the bond between mother and baby.

Diane was busily preparing the evening meal. When they entered the house, she was all smiles. "Say, what is this I hear from my friend, Gloria? Why didn't you tell me, Cox? This is *so* exciting!"

"What are you talking about, Diane," Charles inquired.

"Do you mean to tell me that you two have been together all afternoon, and he hasn't told you that he proposed to Gloria this morning? I don't believe it!"

This caught the attention of everyone in the house. Charles was especially elated.

"This is a time to celebrate! Break out the Champagne. I want to propose a toast!"

"You know we don't drink Champagne, but I have some grape juice. Will that do?"

Excitement filled the house as she poured glasses of grape juice for everyone and they began to toast Cox and congratulate him. He was beside himself with joy.

"What a day this has been," he told Shep as he drove home that evening. His life was becoming more and more complicated every day, but it was a positive change from the past years of boredom and loneliness.

He carried a bucket of water from the well and put it on the hotplate to heat. He needed to take a bath, if you could call it a bath, and wash out some socks and underwear. Tomorrow was Saturday. He and Gloria had a standing date every Saturday night and for church on Sunday.

As he rubbed his socks together in the soap suds, he began to daydream of Gloria walking down the church aisle to take his hand in marriage. He tried to picture her with a long, flowing veil on her head and a colorful bouquet of flowers in her hand. He knew she would have that beautiful smile. She *always* had that beautiful smile.

A HEALING TALK

Charles waited until they were alone to discuss the problem of Marlin. He was careful to avoid any criticism of Diane. He knew she was having a hard time maintaining a positive attitude. She was trying to keep up with the garden, picking, canning, and freezing produce every day, plus trying to keep three meals on the table for the family. She wasn't feeling well much of the time, either. Kendra and Mark were a big help to her but there was a lot they couldn't do yet.

"Honey, I'm concerned about Marlin. Have you noticed a change in him lately?"

"Yes, I have noticed that he doesn't seem to be the same happy youngster he used to be. I thought he might just be tired from all the work he's trying to do. He never stops."

"I know. It's like he thinks he has to earn his keep, or earn our affection, or both."

"He should know better than that. We both love him. He is such an unusually good kid."

"He has had a pretty difficult childhood. It probably stems from that." Charles added.

"What do you think we can do to make things better?" Diane asked.

"Do you think it would help if we sat down with him and talked it out? We could encorage him to tell us exactly how he feels. That would give us an oppertunity to reassure him that we like having him here."

Diane was silent as she readied herself for bed. Then, with tear filled eyes she said, "I haven't been treating that boy right. I've spoken harshly to him when he didn't deserve it. It seems that I want to blame him for any little thing that goes wrong. I owe him an apology."

Charles took his wife into his arms and soothed her as she cried softly against his shoulder. "Let's have that talk tomorrow, Charles. I hate to have Marlin feeling unwanted here."

The next morning, as was their custom, they were up early, sitting at the table having coffee, when Marlin appeared.

"Here Marlin," Charles said as he pulled another chair away from the table. "Sit here with us. We want to have a little talk."

Marlin looked quizically from one to the other. What could this be about? Have I done something wrong? He silently asked himself. He took the chair, still puzzled, waiting-

"Would you like a cup of coffee?"

"I've never drunk coffee. Mother thought I was too young."

"You're older now. Here, put some sugar and cream in it. It will kill the coffee taste," Charles suggested with a smile.

Marlin pulled the cup of coffee closer and added sugar and cream to it. He stirred it slowly, and waited.

Diane started with, "Marlin, I want to apologize to you. I have been short and cranky with you lately, when there was no reason for it. I'm asking you to forgive me."

He studied her face for a few seconds. Tears filled his eyes. "Its okay, Diane. I know you haven't been feeling well. I forgive you."

They both stood up simultainsly and reached for the other. They embraced, fighting back tears, and sat down again. A few minutes passed as they slowly sipped coffee.

It was Charles who spoke now. "Marlin, we both are aware that your feeling about being here with us has changed lately, and we're real sorry that has happened. We want to give a chance tell us exactly how you feel. Don't worry about us getting upset at what you say. We won't do that. We *want* to know. We want to correct any wrong we have done. We love you and want to keep you here as long as you like. Do you understand?"

Marlin was uncomfortable with being the focus of their undivided attention all of a sudden. He didn't know how to respond. He squirmed in his chair and studied his coffee, avoiding eye contact with them. There was a long silence as they waited.

"I, ah, I ah, I don't know what to say. You took me in and treated me like your own. How could I find any fault with that? I am, ah, I

93

appreciate that. I guess I let my feelings get hurt too easily. I'm sorry, Diane, really I am. It's not all your fault. You have been good to me." Looking up, their eyes met in understanding and forgiveness.

Charles heaved a big sigh of relief. "Good," he said. "I guess that kind of clears the air, doesn't it? All is forgiven and we have a fresh start, right?"

Kendra and Mark came bounding down the stairs looking for breakfast, so the routine of the household was restored, as Diane broke eggs into the skillet and dropped bread into the toaster.

This thing about Marlin's mother's place kept gnawing at Sheriff Baker. He didn't want that drunken Bert Simpson to steal it from Marlin, especially knowing how he had mistreated the boy, as well as his mother. He decided to check a little farther into it.

He was driving the offical vehicle down Main Street when he caught sight of Bert entering the local liquor store. He shook his head in disgust as he made a U turn and drove back and parked in front of the courthouse.

The Registrar of Deeds was accustomed to seeing the sheriff and knew him well. "Hello Sheriff Baker. How may I help you today?" she asked.

"I was checking on the Carol Simpson real estate. If it is registered to her son, who is paying the taxes on it since she died and he is gone?"

She thumbed through a filing cabinet and removed a paper file. After studying it for a moment she said, "The taxes are paid for last year but will be due again in December. It would be Marlin's responsibility, since the property is in his name. I don't have a current address for him so I don't know what will happen at that time."

The sheriff thanked her and left. He figured he would just let it go for awhile and see what changes were made between now and December. There really wasn't anything he could do about it anyway, until someone filed a complaint or something. He wasn't sure just how it could be handled. This was something for a lawyer to look into.

He had barely parked in front of his office when Cox pulled in beside him. They stood between their vehicles visiting, when Sheriff Baker reached out his hand and said, "Congratulations, Cox! I know you two will be very happy together. Say, after you get married, you could get Marlin to live with you. Is that your plan?"

"I haven't discussed that with Gloria, although I have thought a lot about it. He is doing real well with the Goodwins though, so I wouldn't want to uproot him again."

"Have you set a date yet?"

"No, we haven't. I think it would be best to wait until the lawsuit is settled and I have some money. I don't want to feel like a gigolo."

"Have you heard any more on that yet?"

"I just came from the legal office. They keep telling me it will be settled soon, whatever that means. I guess I'm impatient. I just want to get my life moving again."

"I can understand that. I hope it will be soon." He stepped to the pickup window and patted Shep on the head. "How's he doing for you?"

"Let me tell you Sheriff. That dog is the *best*. I really appreciate you getting him for me. He is a real companion. I wouldn't want to be without him, for sure. I love that dog!"

"I knew you would like him. Who wouldn't? He is a great dog, aren't you, Shep?"

The dog wagged his tail like a flag waving patriot. He enjoyed all the love and attention from both men.

School had started and the two Goodwin children and Marlin were all outfitted in new clothes, book bags and books as well as paper, pens, pencils and notebooks. Everything on the list in the local paper had been purchased. Marlin was excited. It had been quite a while since he had been in school and he had missed it.

The garden had all but finished producing. The vegetables had been canned, frozen, stored, or eaten. The rest was left to go to seed. Diane had had enough. She was in the second trimester now and still wasn't feeling well. She was glad to be done with the garden and have the kids in school. Now she could relax a little. Even though this baby was a surprise, they were happy about it. She had plenty of time to prepare the nursery.

Time passed quickly, relatively speaking, for Diane. Gloria Strong was planning a baby shower for her at her house and had invited all the neighbor women to take part. It would be a joyous occasion, with many gifts and good wishes. She loved hosting things like this. It was late October when they had learned via a sonogram that the baby was a girl, so everything was done in the traditional shades of pink, highlighted with every color of the rainbow. From the invitations to the table decorations, it was perfect.

After the three children left for school that morning, Diane began the routine of cleaning the kitchen, when suddenly she became light headed, and then everything went black as she collapsed to the floor. Charles had left the house to do his rounds of checking cattle, feeding and working on the farm equipment. Ordinarily he would be gone until noon, but he suddenly felt a strong urging to check on his wife. She had been doing okay, but he had not forgotten the spell she had earlier in her pregnancy. He believed the urging was from the Lord, so he walked briskly to the house. Upon entering, he saw her lying on the floor, unconscious. He rushed in and fell on his knees by her side calling her name. But she did not respond. He wet a cloth and began to wipe her face gently, saying, "Diane, Diane!"

Her eyelids fluttered, and then with a look of utter confusion, she said, "What happened?"

"Are you all right? How do you feel? Here, let me help you up." He lifted her to her feet and then to a chair. "Are you all right?" Charles asked again.

"I think so," she replied. I'm just a little dizzy."

"We'd better go see the doctor, just to make sure."

"But the baby shower is today. I can't miss that!"

"I'll call and see if we can get you in to see the doctor and out in time to go to the shower. Okay?"

He had already picked up the phone and soon they were on their way. The doctor got them right in and checked her over. He questioned her about how hard she was working, if she had been lifting too much, had there been any unusual stress in her life? Have you had any spotting, etc., etc?

96

There seemed to be no reason for the difficulty and the baby was fine. "Just take it easy. Get plenty of rest, and let me know if you have anything unusual going on. I think you will be fine. If this happens again, we may have to put you on complete bed rest until the baby is born."

Time was running short, so they drove directly to Mrs. Strong's house. There were a number of cars already there. Everyone expressed concern for her health and wished her well. Charles, feeling a little out of place, left and would return for her later.

Cox was just entering the driveway when Charles arrived home. The two friends walked together to the machinery shed where Charles had been working on his mowing machine. They chatted as they worked. It was such a pleasure to have a friend like this who had the same interests and didn't mind lending a hand with whatever work you happened to be doing. It was so much better to be able to visit and work than to sit and visit. Charles told him about the problem Diane had had and ask about Cox's lawsuit.

Cox always asked about how Marlin was doing in school, as well as how it was working out at home. They had a mutual interest in the boy.

It had been cloudy and threatening all day. Suddenly, there was a rumble of thunder, then bright lightning, followed by a loud clap of thunder that shook the building.

"Wow!" Charles exclaimed glancing at his watch. "I'd better go get Diane before we have such a downpour we can't get up the hill. Come with me, Cox."

The rain began to come in torrents. They were drenched to the skin by the time they got to the car, but Charles knew he needed to get up the hill to Mrs. Strong's quickly. It was only seven miles away, but it took them fifteen minutes to make the drive. The road was slick and dangerous as water was flowing over it in several places already. Most of the women had gone, as they had been cautioned about the possibility of flash flooding.

Mrs. Strong was waiting under the patio cover watching the rain and looking for Charles. She motioned to them to come in the house. They sprinted through the heavy rain and stood dripping wet under the patio cover. The wind had come up from the east, making the air almost cold. In fact, being wet to the skin, as they were, it *was* cold.

The guests and Diane joined the men on the patio. Gloria gathered up some of her late husband's jackets and some dry shirts for the men to put on. They all watched the rain as it continued to pour down and run in little streams across the driveway and down the road. Occasionally, the lightning and thunder were frightening, but they waited for a break in the storm, hoping to make a run for home.

The sheriff was called to verify the road conditions. He advised them not to get in any hurry. "The rain should be stopping within the hour, but let the water run off the road before you go anywhere. We have had to rescue several people already, because they were in a hurry to get someplace. Ask yourself, "Is getting there right away worth risking my life?"

"You may as well make the best of it. Sit down here, Charles and Cox. I have some cake and tea left from the shower. I'll get you some," Gloria invited.

The little group gathered around the patio table, eating and visiting. It proved to be an enjoyable afternoon. Diane was feeling fine now, and displayed all the gifts she had received for the baby.

The rain stopped, the sky cleared and the sun shone brightly. The abrupt change seemed almost unreal. Soon everyone wanted to get on the road. Cautiously Charles, Diane and Cox took the lead. There were numerous wash-outs across the gravel road, some still running water, but by going very slowly, they reached the main road safely.

TESTING, TESTING...

Day after day, week after week, month after month, Cox checked with the attorneys and waited for some encouraging word about the lawsuit, but there was always some delay. There was nothing he could do but wait a while longer. He had waited twenty eight years already while his life seeped away through the cracks of the so called "justice" system, and now he was waiting again. He consoled himself with the knowledge that at least this time he had *hope*. Still, it was hard to wait when he felt that his years were numbered.

It was December now, and the personal property taxes were due. His own taxes were not very high and he would be selling his calves right away. He was thinking about the taxes on Marlin's property. He didn't know how that would be handled if they didn't have an address for the boy. Who would pay the taxes? He decided he would make it his business to find out. He drove to the courthouse, mounted the steps and found the door bearing the sign "Registrar of Deeds."

"Good morning," the clerk called out cheerfully. "How may I help you today?"

Cox explained his interest in the situation, being careful not to appear "nosey," but concerned. The clerk explained that she had been a close friend to Carol Simpson and was well aware of her husband's mistreatment of Carol and her son. She too was concerned about the property, knowing that it rightfully belonged to Marlin. They had heard about him leaving home under such a terrible threat but that he had found a good home and was happy there. No, they didn't have an address for him. If they sent him a tax statement, how would he pay the taxes? They were in a dilemma, as well.

Cox gave the Wilcox address to the clerk. He determined to discuss it with Charles before the mail reached them. They would decide how to handle it from there. Then he drove over to the Attorneys office to see what was going on, as usual. If it works out, he thought, I'll ask about this as well.

Attorney Wilkins and Attorney Hatfield were together, going over some papers when he was ushered into the inner office. They were excited to see him, which indicated good news.

"Come in Cox. This is good timing. We were just about to call you. We finally got the lawsuit settled. You are now a wealthy man!"

Cox was stunned. He had waited until he had all but given up, and now that they were saying it had happened, he couldn't take it in. His mind refused to accept it. His memory flashed back to the day he was told he had been cleared of murder and was free to leave the prison. At first he thought someone was playing a cruel joke on him. If he believed it, then they would laugh and say, "April fool!" or some such thing.

He stood staring at them, his mind reeling. He was unaware of his surroundings. Mr. Wilkins kept saying, "Mr. Cox. Mr. Cox. Can you hear me, Mr. Cox?" Then he touched his arm, saying, "Are you all right, Mr. Cox? Do you want to sit down, Mr. Cox?"

"Yes, yes, I'm okay." He moved to a chair and dropped heavily into it. "What did you say? It's over? The waiting is over? You got the money for me?" He rubbed his forehead as if trying to stimulate his faltering brain to function again.

"You heard correctly. It's over. We have the money!" They were elated but seemed to understand Cox's reluctance to believe it.

"I don't know what to say. I don't know what to do. I don't know what to think...."

"We understand how you must feel. You don't have to make any decisions about it just now. If you want to talk to a financial advisor, that would be a good thing. Your money is safe until you are ready for it."

He stood now, unsteadily, and studied the men who had "gone to bat" for him. "I thank you boys very much for all the work you have done to make this day a reality for me. I can never thank you enough!" He shook hands all around and left with the intention of getting some sound financial advice from his siblings, his friends and perhaps a financial advisor. The check from the Blumfield estate would be in safe keeping until his head was clear and he was ready to take possession of it. He was trembling with excitement, so much that he was almost afraid to drive. He walked up the street to find Sheriff Baker.

The sheriff was out, so Cox decided to drive on out to see Gloria. He would rather she be the first to know the good news anyway. She was working in the yard, clearing the flower beds of debris. She welcomed him with her winning smile. She knew instantly that something good had happened.

He rushed to her, threw his arms around her and began whirling her around as if she were a little girl, excitedly exclaiming, "We got it! We got it Gloria, we got it!"

When he stopped so that she could speak, she asked, "You got the settlement from the lawsuit? Oh Cox, that's wonderful!"

He leaned forward and did an animation of cranking an old vehicle, saying, "Varrrroooom. Varrrroooom! My life is starting again! Gloria, I'm going to buy you a great big diamond ring and we're going to tie the knot! What do you say to that?"

"I'll tell you what I say, Mr. Cox. I say, YES, YES, YES!" They embraced again and walked to the house with their arms around one another, as exited as any pair of youngsters on Christmas Eve. They sat and sipped tea and made plans for their wedding, for the boys' ranch and for a shopping trip to the city where they had a wide variety of diamond rings to choose from.

Cox brought up the subject of where they would live after the wedding. He explained to her how he felt about not taking advantage of the situation. She was adamant that they should live in her house. "It's the only sensible thing to do. I don't want to move and if I did, what would I do with my place? I can't bear the thought of selling it or renting it out."

"I don't want your children to think that I am marrying you for your possessions..."

"Nor do I want your siblings to think I am marrying you for your money, Cox"

"We could have a pre-nuptial agreement drawn up if you think we should."

"I can't see that it is necessary, but if our families would be more comfortable with that, we could do it. It can always be changed later if we decide to."

Cox asked her to accompany him up north to meet his two brothers and his sister. He would call and make the arrangements. He hoped to have a big family get together and a long talk about what to do with the money. They could talk to them about the pre-nuptial agreement as well.

He wanted to buy a better vehicle and a cattle trailer right away. He needed their help with that decision as well.

After leaving Gloria's, he went to see Charles and Diane. The couple was enjoying a relaxing afternoon watching a movie on T. V. It was a good time of year on the ranch. The summer's work was finished, the children were in school and it was too early to be concerned about baby calves being born. Charles was spending more and more time with Diane, just in case she needed him.

They were always glad to see Cox. He had become one of their dearest friends. The movie was over and they had time to talk. Cox didn't quite know how to tell them the good news. Finally, in a calm matter-of-fact voice he said, "Well, Charles, I don't know how to say this, but you are now looking at a millionaire."

"Is that right?" Charles responded nonchalantly. Then realizing what Cox had said, he jumped up and shouted, "Millionaire? Are you kidding me? They got the settlement? You are truly a millionaire?"

"That's right! I just found out this morning."

Charles thrust out his big right hand saying, "Put 'er there, Pal! Congratulations! I'm so happy for you!"

Diane joined in the fray with congratulations and good wishes. It was a truly joyous time. "Does Gloria know?" She asked.

"Yes, she does. I told her I'm going to buy her a great big diamond ring, and then we will tie the knot."

"I can hardly wait to hear about it from her." Diane added happily.

Later, as Cox and Charles made the rounds checking the cattle, Cox told him about the property belonging to Marlin.

"Now that I will have some money, I'll be glad to pay the taxes on it for him so he won't lose it, but I don't know what can be done about that rat Bert living there. It doesn't seem right to me after the way he treated Marlin and his mother. I was going to talk to the attorneys about it today, but sort of got "side-tracked," he said with a smile.

"I'll watch the mail for the tax bill. When it comes I suppose we'll have to talk to him about it. He probably has no idea the place is his. By that time, you may know what we can do to get Bert off the premises."

"I just wanted to give you a "heads up" before it came in the mail. By the way, I'm looking for some wisdom and guidance as to what to do with that money. Do you have any suggestions?"

"Are you still planning to start a boy's ranch? If you are, that will take a good share of it."

"Yes, Gloria and I are, but until we get organized and find the right property, we need a safe place to invest it."

"I really don't have any expertise in that area, Cox."

The school bus pulled in and the kids piled out. Cox thought it was a little strange to see Marlin without the hat and boots. The boy rushed straight to him for a hug. The other two ran to the house to see their mother and to check for snacks.

Cox arranged to have the money divided between several banks in the area for temporary safe- keeping. He had a good sized piece put into a checking account, so he could repay his brothers, pay his taxes, and purchase a pickup and stock trailer. Above all, he wanted to buy Gloria that diamond engagement ring. Never in his life had he had an opportunity to spend that kind of money and he was nervous. Fortunately, Gloria had had some experience with money. She would be a big help to him.

His brothers, Chip and Rush, had agreed to meet him at their sister Laura's house. The whole family would be there. They had not been told about the settlement yet, but his tone of voice indicated a turn around in his life. They had no idea he had met the love of his life and would be married soon.

They drove Gloria's car, so everyone was doubly surprised, first by the car, then by the lady on Cox's arm. What a splendid, happy day it was! His family didn't know if they were happier because of Gloria or because of the settlement their brother so richly deserved.

After a wonderful meal, they discussed Cox's plans for the boys home; how to organize it, finance it, staff it, etc. Gloria was the expert in this, as she had had so many years experience doing it, but she was very humble, allowing all of them to have input. As she said, "No one knows it all and one can always learn from another." They all appreciated her attitude and loved her.

Next, they discussed vehicles; what make was best for the price, etc. Who knows about a suitable one for sale, and where to find a good used stock trailer? Cox wanted to be frugal with the money. Then they discussed jewelry stores.

They would shop for a pickup truck first. It was a "shopping party" of sorts, with a parade of vehicles going from dealership to dealership, comparing prices, test driving and just plain having fun.

Cox made the remark, "I wonder if this would be so much fun if I had had a normal life before?"

They settled on a white, five year old GMC pickup with red pen stripes down the sides. Cox paid for it with a check and a smile. As they drove off together, Gloria expressed her admiration for the way he handled the whole affair. "Just like a pro," she said proudly.

Now it was time to find a stock trailer. That wasn't difficult, as there were only two dealerships in the area. They settled on a white twenty-four foot trailer that had recently had the floor replaced with oak lumber. It would be more than adequate for his little herd, but he planned to have a bigger spread and more cattle in the future.

With the pickup and trailer bought, they all returned to Laura's. Her brothers returned to their homes, as well as all the grandkids and a few great grandchildren. It had been one of the best days of his life, Cox said, and he had been having a number of good days lately. Cox and Gloria would spend the night at Laura's, and then go shopping for the ring on the morrow.

Being morning people anyway, the whole household was having breakfast at 6:00 AM

A list had been compiled of all the jewelry stores in the area and the ones recommended by various family members. They were well prepared, as they drove away to shop for that special diamond ring.

Traveling from town to town was proving to be very time consuming, so the couple gave that up and decided to shop in Allentown. They were familiar with the streets and some of the stores anyway. They found a little "mom and pop" type store on the corner of Main Street, and to their surprise they had in stock several beautiful rings they both liked... They were less costly than the big name brand stores, so they were pleased by that. The two were finding that they were like minded on most everything.

Gloria pointed out three rings she liked and said she would go sit in the car while he made the choice. That way it would be something of a surprise to her. Cox struggled with the decision. He would rather she had done it, but he wanted to please her in whatever she wanted. He took the most expensive one, not because he thought it was prettier or better, but because he really couldn't choose. He wrote a check for it, being very careful to do it correctly, even though it took a little extra time. Then he asked them to gift wrap it.

They had agreed that he would give it to her on their next date. Being older people, they had learned that anticipation is sometimes better than the actual experience. Instant gratification was left to the young.

Gloria held the pretty little gift package admiringly all the way back to Laura's place. After visiting briefly she left in her car while Cox proudly drove his new pickup, pulling the trailer back down the road. It was a good one hundred miles back, but he didn't mind at all. This is about as good as it gets, he thought. He had left Shep with Charles so that gave him an excuse to show off his new stuff when he stopped to get him.

Marlin was as excited about the new rig as Cox was. Charles admired the purchase from end to end. Cox beamed with pleasure, but didn't hesitate to let Shep ride in the cab. This was his buddy.

When he arrived home he backed the trailer into the driveway. It took quite a long while as he had no experience at backing a trailer. It tried his patience, backing, pulling forward, backing, pulling forward

105

again and again. It was a good thing there was so little traffic on the road. He decided he would have to find an open space and practice the art of backing, rather than to become embarrassed when he went to a sale barn or some other public place.

He unhitched the trailer so that the pickup would be ready to go tomorrow. He walked all around it one more time, reveling in the ownership of such a vehicle.

===============

The calves were ready to go to market. He had already separated them from their mother and they were weaned, but he had no loading chute. Now that he had the livestock trailer to haul them, he needed a chute of some sort. He began to gather the necessary tools and supplies early the next day. By noon, he had it complete. The next chore was to back up the trailer to the chute. After eating some lunch he drove to the open area he had chosen for a practice field and began to try to back. He set up some empty buckets for markers, but it wasn't as easy as he had hoped. He worked for an hour at it and got quite frustrated before he finally was satisfied with the way it was going. Now he was ready to back up to the chute. He tied the gate open, lined up and began to reverse. He tried three times before he got it right, then heaved a big sigh of relief and cut the engine. He would load the calves in the morning and haul them to the sale.

Of course he had to call Gloria and find out what was going on with her. As they talked she asked if she could go along tomorrow to the auction sale. It had been a long time since she had been to one and she missed it. He was more than pleased to have her go along. She would drive over to his place and they could leave from there.

Cox was out early loading the calves. He only had thirteen and they were gentle and easy to handle. It didn't take long to load them, so he was ready and waiting when Gloria came. It was an uneventful day but an enjoyable one. He collected his check and they drove back to his place. He hesitated about inviting her in as the little place was no prize, but she was curious to see the house anyway. Apologizing, he held the door for her to enter. "It is only a bachelors hut, but it's been home for a year now. I'm looking forward to the day I'll be living in a nice house with a wise and wonderful wife. Do you know where I might get one?" he kidded.

"If you look any farther than right here, you're in deep trouble, Mr. Cox!" she replied emphatically. "I see you keep it neat and clean. I'm impressed."

"It's not the place a man would want for his bride."

"People have started out with a whole lot worse, Cox," she reminded him.

"Would you be interested in driving down to Bucklin? I want to deposit this check and see what I can find out about Marlin's home place."

"Sure, I'd like to see the place."

They took Gloria's car and drove south to the little town. Cox pointed out all the land marks he had learned, such as the sheriff's office, the courthouse, the bank and the real estate office. They drove on south to the little place where Marlin grew up. Cox was surprised to see that it had overgrown with weeds and grass and there were no curtains on the windows. "It looks abandoned," he remarked.

"It does look abandoned. Let's pull into the driveway and look inside," she suggested.

They went up the walk and tried the door. It opened, and to their surprise, the place was a mess! It looked like it had been ransacked. They went from room to room and every one was cluttered. They checked the closets and cabinets and found them empty except for the closet in the master bedroom. It was full of ladies clothing. They assumed they were Carol's.

"It looks like he has moved out and left the trash behind. I wonder what's up with that."

"I have no idea but I think we should try to find out. If he is gone, we need to secure the place for Marlin before vandals destroy it," Cox added.

They closed the door and drove into town. After depositing the calf check they went to a little cafe for lunch. Afterward they found the sheriff and ask if he knew anything about what was going on out there. "No, I don't know. It seems a little strange though. Come to think of it, I haven't seen him going to the liquor store lately. I know some people who were friendly with him. We could ask them about him. Follow me and we'll drive over there."

Several blocks west they turned and parked at the curb. The sheriff walked to a little run down house and knocked. A woman came to the door wearing a ragged house coat. They talked briefly and the sheriff returned. "Mrs. Parks says he was going to sell the place but found out he had no right to it, so he left. He had met some woman from Allentown and they were going to live together. I'd say that's a pretty good outcome as far as Marlin is concerned. He won't have to have the devil evicted. Did he tear the house up?"

"No, fortunately he didn't. He just left trash and things he apparently didn't want."

The sheriff removed his hat and scratched his head thoughtfully. "If it was cleaned up it could be rented out pretty easily. It seems like every body and his brother wants to live outside of town where they can have a horse or something."

"I think we should go back out there and change the locks and make it more secure until we talk to Marlin and see what he wants to do with it. It would be better to have some responsible person living there than to have it setting empty." Gloria said.

So they went to the hardware store and bought locks and a screwdriver and went to work. Gloria returned to her place and left Cox washing out the stock trailer.

Cox turned all night in his bed like a revolving door. He was so elated about the way his life was going. He had so many plans to work out; the details were driving him frantic. He just didn't have the answers to the how, where, who, what and when.

Uppermost on his mind was getting married. He hadn't given the ring to Gloria yet, so he wanted to set a date with her right away. He wanted to handle everything the right way. We also needed to take time to talk to Charles and Marlin about the house. And then there was the dream of having a home for needy boys.

If I'm going to do this, I need to get started, he told himself, and I do want to do it. Otherwise my life will have no meaning. I do want to make a difference with the time I have left and with the money I have been awarded. He decided he would talk to Gloria the first thing tomorrow morning.

================

On the telephone the next day, he explained what he had in mind and how he needed her help. He gathered his notes together and drove to her house. Soon they were seated at the table, elbow deep in papers and pencils. They compiled a list of people who had volunteered to help with the project. They choose several people to act as board members and advisors. They called them and set up a meeting. From that meeting, Cox hoped to have ideas as to how to get the necessary license, permits, etc., and then they could begin looking for a suitable place for the ranch. He was still thinking about the Kester place.

Setting that aside, they began talking about their marriage plans. Cox was in a hurry, but Gloria, knowing that one never really *knows* another as well as one thinks, suggested they get pre-marriage counseling from the pastor. Wanting to save themselves from as many problems as possible down the road, Cox readily agreed. That would take six weeks, which would put the wedding date somewhere after the first of March. The Wilcox baby was due in February and they wanted Charles and Diane to stand up with them, so they needed to confer with them.

"Cox, you have never talked much about what it was like living in prison. Would you mind telling me about that experience? Gloria asked.

"It's a hard thing to talk about. I would like to blot it out of my mind forever, but I know that's impossible. Talking about it brings up a lot of ill will, hurt feelings, hatred and regret. The total frustration of it all is the worst part. If I had actually done something deserving of prison, I think it would have been easier to endure and to forget."

"I can understand that. I don't want to cause you any additional problems by asking about it. I thought it might help ease the pressure to talk about it. I hate to think that you are like a pressure cooker, keeping all this to yourself. You could blow your cork some day."

"There was a time when I felt like a pressure cooker, but the Lord released the pressure when I turned it over to Him. I will tell you that it is probably the worst place a person could ever be, in the land of the brave and free. I know that in some foreign countries it is much worse. They are allowed to torture the inmates and the places are filthy and infested with vermin. I get that it could have been much worse. The hardest part for me was the isolation. To be completely cut off from my family or any one from my past was devastating. When the mail was delivered, there was never a letter for me. I didn't have a single visitor in all those years. The loneliness seeps into your very bones. The endless days and nights run into endless weeks and endless months and years. You loose track of time. After awhile you don't know what day it is or even what year. If you are to be there for life, what difference does it make? I didn't have a life sentence but to me it was the same thing. Then there is the cruelty and the deception of the men around you, not only the inmates, but also the guards and other personal. You can't really trust any of them. You can't relax. You have to be on guard twenty four/seven. The yelling, swearing, insulting, filthy talk, lying, and threats never end. On top of all that is the drugs they manage to get smuggled into the place. Men die every day from overdosing on drugs and not all of it is one's own doing, if you know what I mean. The walls, the bars, the banging doors are a continual reminder that you are not free. It is a totally joyless place. Being a prison inmate drains a person of humanity. Yet in all this, Jesus Christ stands with open arms, inviting us to come to him so that He can "make it all better." I've seen some of the hardest criminals fall to their knees in tears and stand again, completely changed. It is amazing! And He even changed me."

Cox was visibly moved by the memories of what he endured in prison. Talking about it did help in one way, but remembering grieved his soul...

"Thank you, for sharing that with me, Cox. For a change of pace, would you like to drive over to see Diane and Charles? Maybe we can work out something on a wedding date."

Shep sat in the pickup bed as the couple drove down the hill to visit their friends. The weather was cold as it was now January. A light snow was falling and the wind was kicking up. The forecast warned of heavy snow. The visit would be short, allowing everyone to be home in their own cozy place before it began to fall.

The three youngsters eagerly gathered around the large table to hear the latest plans.

"Before we discuss the wedding, Gloria and I have some good news for Marlin."

Marlin looked quickly from one to the other, trying to imagine what this could be about. Cox continued, "We drove by your home place today and it has been abandoned."

"Abandoned? Marlin asks in surprise. You mean Bert is gone? He's not there anymore?"

"That's right. He moved out, lock, stock and barrel. We talked to Sheriff Baker about it and he didn't have any information, but he knows some folks Bert hung around with, so we drove to their place. The sheriff talked to the lady and found out that he had planned to sell the place but found that he couldn't so he moved to Allentown to live with his girlfriend. All he left is trash and what we figured is your mother's clothes."

"Wow, that's great that he's gone, but I can't go and live there by myself. What will we do with it?" Marlin asked.

"The sheriff thinks you could easily rent it out. Of course it will have to be cleaned up first. The grass and weeds had about taken over. He must have been gone quite awhile."

"If you put the rent money away it would help you quite a bit when you get ready to go to college. Someday you might want to get married and live there with your bride," Gloria suggested.

"That sounds like a good idea," Diane said. "You will have come full circle. That would be a long road home."

We will all work out those plans with you as we go along, Marlin. Right now, we have some other plans to work on," Cox stated.

They discussed the baby's arrival, the wedding date and the snow falling outside. The baby was due the first day of February. Diane would be back to her original figure, hopefully, by the middle of the month, so she would be glad to stand with Gloria. They tentatively set the date for March 7th. That would allow time for the counseling to take place, the invitations to go out, the flowers to be bought, etc. They wanted all the children to have a part as well. Kendra could be a flower girl and the boys could be ushers. Everyone was pleased with the arrangements, so far, anyway.

Later that night, Cox wrestled with his memories. He thought of all the young men who had been brought into the prison and had to endure terrible sexual attacks from the older inmates. Some were unable to fight them off. Their screams tormented Cox. He had tried to defend some of them and had been beaten as a result. He spent numerous nights in the infirmary as a result. He tried to turn those memories off and to dream of the wedding and being married to Gloria. The conflict in his mind kept him awake for hours. He went to the Lord in prayer. God was his refuge, his ever present help in any kind of trouble.

THE JANUARY BLIZZARD

Marlin awakened in the night to the sound of wind blasting the house. It came in great gusts. Something had come loose from the house and was banging back and forth with every wind gust. He got out of bed and looked out the window. The snow had piled up in huge drifts across the driveway between the house and the equipment barn. He couldn't see well enough to tell if they would be able to open the door or not, so he quietly went downstairs and looked out the window. The drift almost covered the window. He looked out the little diamond shaped window in the door, or tried to. He couldn't see anything. It was covered with snow. He opened the door and saw that a snow drift was banked up to the top of the storm door. He went to the back door which was on the east side of the house. It was clear of snow, but the drifts were as high as his head. He became concerned about the livestock. He didn't know whether to awaken Charles or not. He looked at the clock on the kitchen range. It was flashing 12:00 o'clock. In the dinning room there was a battery operated clock so he checked it. It read 4:30 o'clock.

The wind was howling and the loose siding, or whatever it was, banged louder. He went to the door of Charles and Diane's bedroom and knocked softly. There was no response. He slowly opened the door. Both of them were sound asleep and Charles was snoring. He went to that side of the bed and put his hand on Charles' shoulder and spoke his name. Charles was startled out of sleep. "What? What? Who? Marlin! What is it? What's wrong?"

"It's the snow, Charles. It's real deep and blowing into big drifts. I was worried about the animals. I didn't want to wake you up but I thought you should know."

Charles sat up and quickly pulled on his pants and the two went to look out the window again.

"Oh my! Look at that!" Charles exclaimed. He opened the front door just as Marlin had done, then closed it and went to the east entrance. "At least we can get out this door."

I hope the cows didn't drift into the corner of the pasture and get buried in the snow. I don't think there is anything I can do for them yet. As soon as it gets daylight I'll take the tractor and try to get to them. Call Cox and make sure he's okay while I get dressed, will you?"

Marlin dialed the number and waited. It rang six times before Cox answered, "Hello."

"Hi Cox. It's Marlin. Are you alright?"

"Yeah, why wouldn't I be? What are you doing calling me at this time of night?"

"Charles wanted me to call and see if you are okay. The snow is really drifting and we're concerned about the livestock. Our north door is drifted shut but the east one is clear. Can you get out of your house?"

"I don't know. Hold on a minute and I'll see." Marlin heard him shuffle to the door and open it. He had no storm door, so the next thing he heard was a shout of "Oh, no!" as the snow piled into the house and covered half the floor. Cox grabbed the phone and said, "I have a big pile of snow in my house now. I'll call you back when I get the door shut again."

Marlin explained to Charles what happened. "He will be able to take care of himself as long as he isn't trapped in that little house. I need to call Gloria and warn her."

She answered right away and had already been up checking things out. Her patio door in on the south and is protected, so she is alright. Diane has been awakened by all the commotion and is curious to know what it means. "I'll have to take the big tractor out to the pasture and check on the cows as soon as there is enough light. I hope the wind dies down soon. I pray for God's mercy on the poor critters. Only He can keep them safe through this storm. You may as well go back to bed. If I had known this was coming, I could have brought them home where they had shelter. I didn't realize it was going to turn into a blizzard!" He started a pot of coffee and began pacing the floor while praying silently for his livestock. Marlin sat at the table and watched in silence. Charles glanced his way and became aware of Marlin's concern. He sat facing him and with a smile gripped the boy by the shoulders. As they looked steadily into one another's eyes, Charles said, "Marlin, I don't tell you this often, but you are one great kid. I really appreciate you and I'm glad you are here as a part of my family!"

Tears filled Marlin's eyes as he realized the sincerity of Charles affirmation. The two stood up simultaneously and hugged.

"Let's have some coffee" Charles suggested as he began filling two cups. "It should be getting light before long. I may try to go using only the tractor lights if this keeps up."

"If they are bunched up in the corner of the pasture and getting buried in snow, what will you do? How can you help them? Marlin wanted to know.

'I've got the front end loader on the big tractor. I'll use it to get through the drifts and then when I find the cows, I'll try to move the snow away from them and hope they will follow the path I've cut. When they get here, we'll let them into the barn. If there isn't enough room inside, they can get out of the storm by standing on the east side. What ever it takes to save their lives we will do. I sure don't want to lose any of them."

"Are you going to let me help you?"

"Yes. I *need* your help. Kendra and Mark are too small and Diane is- you know..."

"I want to help you Charles."

"I know you do. You *always* want to help." His smile expressed appreciation. It was now six o'clock but still dark. The snow continued to fall and the wind whipped it up into ever higher drifts. Charles became more concerned by the moment. "Go get your warmest clothes on and wear your rubber boots. You can do without the cowboy boots today. Put on two pair of sox and your coveralls."

Charles began to bundle himself up as well. He couldn't wait any longer or he might lose the whole herd. He was really grateful for the tractor cab with a heater. Soon the two left the house to make their way to the equipment shed where the tractor was kept. They waded through deep drifts and had to fight their way through some that were above their heads. It was a cold difficult effort with the wind whipping snow in their faces and covering their clothes. Marlin stayed close behind Charles and wondered if they would ever make it. After about fifteen minutes they did reach the south side, but the snow was banked up against the sliding doors. They went around the corner and stood in the shelter of the building on the east side for a few moments to catch their breath, and then they made their way to the walk door and entered. Charles was looking for some scoop shovels in hopes of moving enough snow to free the doors to open for the tractor. They waited inside the door trying to gain courage to tackle the job.

"Are you ready, Little Buddy?" He asked.

"I'm ready."

They hurried out and braced for the force of the wind as they came around the corner again. Charles quickly began digging the snow away from the doors, but it was difficult. He kept at it and Marlin tried to move it away as fast as Charles scooped it out. After what seemed like an eternity, they had a trench dug that would allow the doors to open wide enough for the tractor to go through. Charles began to push one of them, straining to move it back. Finally it moved a few inches causing the snow drift to break loose as an avalanche burying him against the door. Marlin cried out, "Charles!" As he began to dig the snow away from the door with his hands, trying to uncover Charles' head. He was frantic. He knew there was no other way to save him. He *had* to do it! He worked with lightning speed and the strength that comes only in a time of crisis. In a matter of a minute or two, he had reached Charles' elbow. Charles had seen the snow coming down on him and had thrown his arms over his head and against the door. That act alone provided an air space for him. He turned his head and gave Marlin a half frozen smile. Marlin kept digging until Charles could move his body a little and finally he could help dig his own legs and feet out of the snow bank. He laboriously climbed out and together they went to the east side and into the walk door, out of the storm.

"Marlin, you just saved my life out there!" He pulled the frightened boy close and hugged him hard. "Thank you!" He said.

Marlin began to sob. He had been too scared to cry before, but now he sobbed with releif. "I'm sorry. I shouldn't be crying at my age."

"Listen boy, you're never too old to cry. Remember that." He hustled toward the doors again, but this time on the inside. "I should have tried it this way before. We all make stupid mistakes," he said as he began pushing and tugging at the door. It still wasn't moving. He found a rope and tied to it so Marlin could add his strength to it. Little by little, it moved back several feet. They then worked on the other door. It took a lot of time and work but they got them open enough for the tractor to pass through. He started it up and began to push the snow out of the doorway and down the drive. Marlin was elated. They had been successful at last. When they reached the east side of the house Marlin jumped down and ran inside to let Diane know what was going on. She was up and concerned about them. They knew there would be no school today so the other two children were allowed to sleep in.

Back in the tractor cab they watched carefully for the cattle. There was a deep rivene running diagonally across the pasture. They hoped the cattle had not gone into it and become buried. They had to be careful not to run the tractor off into it either. Since the wind was blowing from the southwest, they followed the fence along the north side first, expecting the cattle to drift with the wind. They figured right as they began to see the black hides of the cattle almost completely coated with frozen snow. Some of them were lying down buried, while others stood with their hindquarters to the wind, their heads down. It was a sad sight. If they all lived, it would be a miracle. The cattle were accustomed to the tractor bringing feed to them, so they began to move toward it. Charles wanted to make sure all of them got up on their feet so he drove as close as he dared in order to "spook" them into rising. Sometimes it worked and sometimes it didn't. Marlin wanted to jump down and try to get them up, but Charles was hesitant to let him as the wind was so strong and visibility nearly zero, besides the snow being so deep it was hard to walk in it. He eased the scoop of the tractor under the downed cattle one at a time and lifted them gently, encouraging them to stand.

Finally, he had no choice. He and Marlin both jumped down and began to yell and smack the cows to get them going. Charles drove the tractor in front of the cows in order to clear a path for them as well as to give them something to follow. It seemed to be working. Slowly, ever so slowly, the parade moved along toward home. As they neared the barn the cows broke into a run and went into the barn following the path he had cut on his way out to them... Charles went in and tried to count them. Some were still missing. He put out several bales of hay for them and went back to look for the others.

They both strained to see the missing cows. The sun had finally come up but the visibility was still very poor. They followed the fence all the way around the pasture, and then began criss crossing it. Just as they were about to give up the search, they saw a small group huddled together near a plum thicket. They all rushed toward the tractor expecting feed, so very soon they were all safe in the shelter of the buildings

With the cattle fed, they turned to the horse pasture. Charles had five horses at that time. One was only a foal, so they went looking for them. They stood in the corner of their pasture, rump to the wind, and the foal sheltered between them. They readily followed the tractor back to the barn where they were led into the stables and fed.

Now that the livestock was safe, the guys realized how hungry they had become. Using the tractor and front end loader, Charles made short work of clearing the driveway from the road all the way to the pasture. He would clear the front step later. Right now he wanted to eat.

Once inside the house and having his hunger satisfied, his thoughts turned to his wife. She was eight and a half months pregnant and could go into labor at any moment. What would he do if she started right now? He would be unable to get her to the hospital. Would he know how to help her deliver the baby at home? He didn't even want to think about such a thing. He reached for the telephone and dialed the county road and bridge department. He explained the situation to them and gave his address. They were out clearing the roads but it was still snowing. The wind had died down but it would be several days before all the school bus routs and mail routs would be open. Yes, they would make it a priority to get his road open as soon as possible.

TRAPPED!

Cox had a time of it trying to get the snow pushed out and the door shut again. He couldn't get out of the house to get a shovel so he had to work with whatever he could find. He finally sacrificed the apple box/night stand for his shovel. It worked, to a certain extent. By the time he got it all picked up and put in the trash can and everything else he could find, he was half frozen, the house was cold and he still had to sweep and mop up the remainder. Now it was time to think about his cows. He had fourteen of them out there in the blizzard and they had no shelter at all. He would have to wait until daylight and then decide what to do.

He fixed himself some eggs and toast for breakfast and thought about Gloria. He had planned to have a date with her and put the ring on her finger tonight, but that ws not going to happen now. He went back to bed in hopes of getting warm again. His little wood burning stove couldn't keep up with the need when the wind was blowing.

He slept soundly until mid morning. The sound of heavy equipment on the road awakened him. He reached to turn on the light but the electricity was off. He had an oil lamp for such occasions so he struck a match for light and lit it. He tried to look out the small window, but it was buried in snow. He knew then that he would have to push his way out the door somehow; otherwise he could sufficate in there.

He opened the door a small crack to see if the snow was going to pile in again. All he could see was white. He would need some outside help to get out of the house. He closed it and reached for the telephone, hoping it would work. Another disappointment; it was dead! Now what could he do? He was trapped in his own house!

He began to panic! Pacing the floor he began to cry out to the Lord for help and direction. He went to the little window again and tried to open it. It gave a little so he kept trying. It was on the same wall as the door but several feet farther to the east. Frantically, he worked at it, not concerned about the snow falling inside this time. He got it to open about four inches. He took the broom handle and began poking it into the snow in hopes of getting some air into the house. He poked it in every direction and kept cranking it to make the hole bigger. He began to dig with his hands. The snow was piling up at his feet but he was desperate. He would dig for awhile, and then tug on the window hoping it would open wider. It wasn't working. Eventually, he saw a little daylight in the hole going east. By this time he was feeling light headed and knew he disn't have much time. He took the iron skillet from the hot plate and smashed the window glass. He knocked the shards loose from the sash to prevent getting cut on them, then pulled a chair over to the wall and kept digging into the snow drift. He climbed out as the tunnel grew. He was concerned that the snow above him would fall and bury him. He had a tunnel going along the south wall toward the east. He finally reached the edge of the snow drift but it kept falling, covering the hole he had made. He backed into the house again and began to work with the broom to keep the air vent open. He could have climbed out but, then what? The pickup was likely buried under the snow and if it wasn't, he couldn't get through the drifts anyway. He was better off in the house.

His faithful dog, Shep, lay near the wood burning stove watching the whole process.

"Old boy, Cox said, if I could send you out for help, I would. But you weren't trained for such as that. Anyway, I'd worry about you out there."

Cox was very concerned about the cows, but was helpless to do anything for them. He hoped Charles would come to his rescue when he realized the telephone was out.

Gloria had loaned him some books to read, so he sat down with one of them. Shortly, he heard an engine coming along the road again. He assumed it was the county road and bridge men clearing the road. If only he had some way to let them know the predictiment he was in-

Time was dragging along, but the book was interesting. He kept clearing the air vent every little while. He couldn't tell if the snow had stopped or not. The wind had at least died down.

About one o'clock in the afternoon, Cox heard what he thought was a tractor pulling into his driveway. Excitedly, he rushed to the window, stuck his head out and yelled, "Hello!" "Hello!" He then quickly tied his red bandana hankerchief onto the broom and stuck it out the air vent. As he wriggled it around he yelled, "Hello!"

Then to his delight he heard Charles yell, "Cox, are you in there?"

"Yes! But I can't get out."

"I see your flag. I'll scoop the snow away from that area first. Are you alright?"

Yes, I'm okay. The phone and electricity are out though."

There was no answer as Charles had already returned to the tractor where Marlin was anxiously waiting. "Is Cox alright?" He asked.

"Yeah, he's fine. He can't get out though, until we move some of this snow away from the house." He lowered the scoop and inched it under the snow, lifted it and hauled it out away from the house and driveway, load after load, until the window was clear of snow.

Cox climbed out and dropped to the ground, grateful to be free again. Marlin came running and gave him a hug saying, "I'm so glad you are okay, Cox!"

"Charles, I thank you so much for coming to my rescue. I would have been in a bad way in a day or two with no firewood and very little food in the house. I might have had to eat 'Ol Shep's dog food."

"What are friends for? Anyway, Marlin wouldn't leave me alone until I came to see about you."

"Were your cows alright?"

"Marlin got me out early to see about them. We had quite a time, but we did get them to come home, so they are all okay. I hope yours all survived."

"I hope so too. They don't have any shelter at all. They may be buried under the snow."

"Let's take the tractor and go see. Get in the cab with us and we'll clear a path to the gate."

The big tractor roared up the trail to the gate, pushing the snow along as it went. They soon had a clear path and Cox jumped down to open the gate. As they drove along they found a few cows here and a few there. All were covered with snow and bogged down in it. Carefully Charles moved the snow away from them, allowing them to move into the cleared path. Three of them were completely buried but their warm breath had melted snow away from their noses so that they could breath. They were very near death, but revived quickly when the snow was removed from in front of them allowing them to get more air.

Charles cleared a circular area for them, piling the snow up as a wind break for them. Then they brought hay from the stack near the house and fed them. It looked like they would all be fine in a few days. Cox could haul them some hay every day and they were intelligent enough to lick up snow for water.

When they returned, Charles pushed the snow away from Cox's pickup and the house. It would be a muddy mess for awhile when the snow melted, but there was hope that all would be well. Cox brushed the snow off the pickup and started it. He wanted to be sure he could get out on the road. He would need to replace the glass in the window right away. After pulling the pickup out to the edge of the road for him, Charles and Marlin returned home.

Cox left for Bucklin to get the glass for his window. He was getting to be quite the handy man since moving here. He was always asking questions and buying tools, trying to learn how to fix something that most men would have already known. But he wasn't ashamed to ask. He had the window fixed in short order and was pleased with the results. He cleaned the snow away from the doorstep and emptied the containers of snow he had setting in the house. He swept it all out and started a fire again. He carried a good supply of wood into the house, then he and Shep drove up the road to see Gloria. He carried the little gift package in his coat pocket, just in case....

It was evening and the power was still off. Gloria had several oil lamps burning as well as a fire in the fireplace. It provided a romantic setting for what was about to take place.

Gloria quickly fixed a simple meal for the two of them. After putting a pretty cloth on the table, she arranged two place settings of fine china and silver ware. She filled two crystal goblets and lit two candles. It was an attractive arrangement. Cox watched with appreciation. Soon they were enjoying a meal together. After clearing the dishes off the table, Cox brought out the little gift package and placed it on the table. "Open it," he said with a smile. She carefully untied the bow, loosened the paper and lifted out the box. "Now it's your turn," she said.

Cox opened the box and held it so she could get a good look inside. "Oh, it is georgious! That is the one I hoped you would choose, Cox." He removed the ring, then taking her left hand in his; he carefully slid it onto her slender finger. Taking both her hands in his, he lifted her to her feet and embraced her. "My one and only Fiancée!" he crooned and kissed her tenderly.

"You are so romantic, Cox. I love you!"

"And I love you, Gloria!"

The two lovers spent a quiet evening together discussing their plans for the future. Then there was the matter of Marlin and his house south of Bucklin.

"I know you would like to have Marlin live with us once we are settled in, but what about the Wilkins? How do they feel about that?"

"More importantly, how do you feel about it? Cox asked.

"I care deeply for the boy and would enjoy having a youngster like that in my household. My only concern is for the Wilkins and of course for Marlin. He may not want to make the change."

"You're right about that. I sure wouldn't want to twist his arm. We'll just have to "play it by ear."

"Someone needs to clean his place up if it's to be rented. You and I could work on that if you like. It isn't a good time for Diane and Charles to try to do much, with the baby coming so soon."

"Yes, we could. I need something more to do anyway. We would get to know each other really well doing a project like that, don't you think?" Cox stated.

"Yes, that's the best way I know. You might change your mind about marrying me before that job is finished," she said with a smile." "I seriously doubt if that will happen, Gloria." "

"If they get the power and the phone working tomorrow, we could call and see about getting together with them tomorrow evening. Let's ask them to come up here. It would be easier on Diane."

Cox left for home feeling very satisfied and happy. He could hardly wait until Gloria was his wife. He had given up the dream of marriage for many years thinking it could never happen, and now to find such a wonderful perfect mate was almost unfathomable.

The meeting with the prospective board of advisors for the boys' ranch was at 10:00 that next morning in the town hall at Bucklin. Five men and one woman came, besides Cox and Gloria. The discussion continued, centered on permits, regulations, and financing for the ranch. All was going well and Cox felt encouraged, until an attorney by the name of Hathaway, who had volunteered his services to get all the legalities worked out, cleared his throat and said, "There is one problem that came up yesterday as I was talking with another attorney from up north. It seems that Mr. Cox here is a convicted felon. It is illegal for a convict to operate any facility for youth such as you propose. Were you aware of that?"

An angry protest erupted from the little group. "Why had the subject even come up?" "Cox had been completely open and above board about his past prison time and all the circumstances," people shouted.

"Why would that even be a consideration since he was proven innocent?" Mr. Barber asked angrily.

"We all knew about his past experience and admire his compassion for the youth in need of help. He is a man of integerity. Mr. Cogburn added.

"According to the law, it doesn't make any difference. He is still a convict even though he is innocent of any crime. The belief is that the influence of the prison environment may have contaminated his character. Add to that the fact that people know he did time, and you have the potential for difficulty in every aspect of the operation."

"That just cannot be right! Where is the justice in such a ruling?"

"I don't make the rules. I'm just telling you what I know."

Gloria's eyes filled with tears. How can they do him so dirty when he is trying to do something so good?

Cox put his arm around her shoulder and spoke in her ear. "There is something fishy about this. I'll have to check it out with the attorneys. They knew my plans and didn't say a word about this. Don't worry, Sweetheart. It's just another bump in the road."

The little meeting became caotic, and had to be dismissed without accomplishing anything. Cox spoke briefly saying "There is some misunderstanding here. Let's dismiss until we can find out what to do about it."

Everyone except Attorney Hathaway crowded around Cox, reassuring him that they would stand behind him in whatever decision he made regarding the boys ranch. Attorney Hathaway slipped out the door and left.

Before going home, Cox stopped by the attorney's office and made an appointment.

He couldn't help feeling hurt and disappointed about what had just happened. The incident was very disturbing, to say the least. He and Gloria decided not to discuss it farther until they had met with the other attorneys. They ate dinner in a cafe before going home. She dropped him off and drove on to her place as he needed to check on his cows.

The melting snow was creating a difficult mess everywhere. The cows were standing ankle deep in it and the cattlemen were worried about footrot. Cox wanted to feed his cows on top of the hill where it was dryer ground, but his pickup couldn't make it through the mud. He drove to town and looked for a small tractor that he could use for feeding and such. He found an old farmall he liked and bought it. Sheriff Baker happened along about that time and offered to drive it home for him. That was a perfect arrangement. He and Shep slowly followed the tractor along the road home. He then drove the sheriff back to his place.

He had a small trailer he could use to carry a few bales of hay. The cows gladly followed the hay up the hill to the fresh feeding ground. Cox's next project was to build them some sort of shelter before another storm hit.

The electric and phone service was restored so the get-together was arranged for that evening. It was a happy time for everyone. The Wilcox children had not often gone to Gloria's house and they were excited.

Marlin couldn't wait for the discussion to get started since he knew it concerned him.

The first order of events was showing off the engagement ring. Diane seemed as excited about it as Gloria was. "It's beautiful! You made a good choice, Cox," she said.

They all sat around the table enjoying homemade cookies and milk when Cox asked, "Marlin, have you thought about what you want to do with your house?"

"Yes, I think I want to do what you said. Rent it out and save the money for college. When I am old enough, I want to live there."

"Gloria and I will clean it up and get it ready to be rented, if you like. It will keep us occupied while we wait for our wedding day," Cox offered.

"That's great! Maybe I can help during Spring break. I'm anxious to see it again."

"You can see it anytime, Marlin," Charles said.

"Then that's settled. I'll pay the taxes on it. Now let's talk about your future, Marlin. Charles and I have already talked about this, so you don't have to worry about hurting someone's feelings. We both think a lot of you and want to keep you, but the choice is yours. You're doing great there with Diane and Charles and if you want to stay there, that's fine, but Gloria and I want to offer you a home with us after we are married and settled in. You don't have to give us an answer tonight. Think about it and let us know later. You have the other kids as brother and sister to you here and we can't offer you that. We only want you to be happy."

Kendra and Mark looked anxious. "We want you to be our brother, Marlin. Don't we Kendra?" Mark asked. "Please Dad, don't let him leave!"

"That will be Marlin's decision. He will have some time to think about it."

"I love all of you, Marlin said. I don't think I *could* choose between you."

"You'll stay where you are for now, at least. We don't want to uproot you anyway. I just want you to know that we care. From the day you came knocking on my door last April, I have tried to think of a way to have you with me, but as long as you are happy here, I'm okay with it.

I'll still come to see you real often. After we are married, we will be living here at Gloria's, so we will be closer to you. Okay?" Cox asked.

"Oh yeah, that's great! When I came down the road that night I had no one. Now I have a brother and sister and two of the best dads and mothers in the world. I must be the luckiest kid alive!"

"I think everythig is settled for now, so we just as well go home, Diane, Kids. Tomorrow is another school day."

They all stood on the patio and chatted for a moment or two, then the family left. Cox and Gloria exchange a few words and Cox took Shep and drove home feeling satisfied with the way his life was going...

=================

The big snow had fallen on Monday. The week had gone by rapidly with so much going on. Now it was Saturday. Cox made a trip to town to buy supplies to build a windbreak for the cows. He would build it near the stack lot so it would be handier to feed them hay. The ground was frozen a few inches down, so it was difficult to dig the necessary post holes. He was thankful for sandy soil. At least it didn't stick to the diggers, the shovel and the tamping bar too badly. He worked several hours, digging the holes and setting the posts. This was the kind of work he had learned to do growing up on his parent's ranch. It brought back many fond memories of working with his father and going in at noon to eat his mother's good cooking. How he missed those good days! Today he would go into his little shack, warm up some canned beans and a skillet baked biscuit and call it dinner.

He wanted to finish the wind-break today so he would be free all day Sunday to go to Church with Gloria and spend the day with her. It was a good incentive to keep at it. He nailed a heavy frame work to the posts, then corrigated tin on that. He nailed another frame on top of the tin to keep it from blowing off or the cows from pushing it loose. By the end of the day, he was satisfied with the job he'd done. Later, he would build a feed bunk behind the windbreak. That should help the cows get through the winter, he thought.

Sunday was spent just as he had planned. It was such a joy to be with Gloria. Of course all the ladies gathered around and gushed with compliments over her ring. Later, they met in the pastor's study for a counseling session. He gave them a test to show their compatibility with one another, which was encouraging as it showed them to be a good match...

"You are off to a good start, the pastor enthuesed. I'll see you next Sunday."

The appointment with the attorneys group was 10:00 o'clock Monday morning. Cox and Gloria arrived early and waited to be called into the office. They were a little aprehensive after what had happened at the meeting last week.

Attorneys Wilkins and Hatfield greeted them warmly. They hadn't met Gloria before and were favorably impressed with her. "You are a very lucky man, Cox." they said.

"I agree. It's about time I had some favor in this crazy world," Cox answered smiling proudly.

"Have a chair and we'll get down to business." Wilkins shuffled some papers on his dest and said, "We have done some research in the matter of you not being qualified to operate youth facality. I couldn't find any law related to that subject. Apparently, Attorney Hathaway used that as an excuse to prolong the process of the youth ranch because of his own misgivings. From what I gather, he wants more time to pass before you go into anything like this. Not because of any character flaw on your part, but because of your being cut off from the outside world for so long. He feels that you need more time to adjust to society."

"If that's the case, he should have said so, rather than to beat around the bush and make untrue statements?" Gloria stated.

"I can't speak for Mr. Hathaway, but I agree that it wasn't the proper way to handle the situation. My recommendation is that you call another meeting with all of them and ask him about it. He needs to show you a law or a precident that gives the authority for such a statement. If he can't, then he needs to just bow out."

"I'm not accusing him of anything, but he seems to be a trouble maker. If he is, we don't need him on the board."

As the couple prepared to leave Attorney Hatfield said, "If you need any farther assistance, don't hesitate to call. We're glad to help out."

While eating lunch at a local cafe, Cox said "I'm having second thoughts about the boy's ranch, Gloria. It may be true that I haven't been out of the joint long enough to prove myself capable of such an undertaking. Maybe we *should* give it more time, especially since we are getting married soon and need time to adjust to living together. I don't want to add any stress to the situation and jeopordize our marriage. What do you think?"

"You really surprised me by saying that, but quite honestly, Cox, I think you are absolutely right! Now I don't think you should give up the dream. Just postpone it for a year or two."

"I'm so glad you agree. I was afraid you would think I was letting that lawyer bully me out of it. I believe what the Word says, "All things work together for good for those who love the Lord and are called according to His purpose." This little incident was for a purpose. It put me to thinking about whether I'm ready for all the responsibility or not. I think we should have another meeting with the board members and tell them what we are thinking. We should encourage them to continue meeting together, planning and promoting the boys ranch. I do hope they can stir up a lot of interest in it and get people wanting to help. It is a big undertaking. I didn't realize how complex it would be until I began to study it."

"That's a good idea. If the community is in favor of it, it will work. If they aren't, we will know to forget it. I've had enough experience with this sort of thing to know how ficle some people are."

"Let's call all the people together one more time this month, then concentrate on our marriage plans. Diane's baby will come soon and I want to be around to help Charles out with the chores."

"Yes, and I am going to help Diane. They are ready, for the most part, but there is always something that needs to be done when there's a new baby coming to the house."

The following Monday morning, the meeting was called to order by Mr. King. When it was opened for any new business, Cox stood and

129

recounted what was said at the last meeting. Afterward he told the group what Attorney Wilkins had found out, or failed to find out.

"Attorney Hathaway, I am not here to cast doubt on what you said at the last meeting about it being contrary to the law for an ex-con to operate a youth facility, whether guilty or not, but to ask for proof of your statements. If that is the law, we will abide by it but, if not I want to know why you made such a statement."

Attorney Hathaway stood and eyed the group momentairly, and then hastily picked up his papers and walked out the door. Everyone laughed aloud. "I guess we know what that means," Mr. Cogburn said.

As the meeting continued, Cox confessed to them the insight the incident had brought to him. They were all understanding and agreed to work together to form a mission statement and to promote the ranch in every possible way for a future date. They would meet once a month to compare notes and get fresh ideas.

THE BABY AND THE WEDDING

Time moved along, sometimes with the speed of humming bird's wings and at other times at a snail's pace. The weather was unpredictable but there were no more big snow storms like the one in January. Diane was looking forward to the baby's birth as she was large and heavy. She wanted to get it over with and get back to normal. She was due in two weeks.

Gloria was busy with her own plans. She wanted to re-arrange the house and remove her late husbands clothes before she and Cox got married. She carefully packed them all in boxes to go to the Salvation Army. It was hard for her as every shirt and every tie- every piece of clothing had a memory attached; He had worn this shirt to their son's graduation, this tie was a gift from his sister, etc. She finally completed the task and stacked the boxes in the spare bedroom. Cox would bring his pickup and help haul them into Allentown.

She wanted to give the master bedroom a fresh coat of paint and hang new drapes, so that it would look entirely different for this new man in her life. The ringing of the telephone brought her back from reminiscing about "Harold and the way it was." "Hello," she said, then listened intently. "Do you need me to come now?" "How close together are your pains?" "Is Charles there with you?" "I'll be right over."

Gloria grabbed her coat, purse and keys and was out the door in a flash. Within minutes she was at Diane's door. "Do you know where Charles is?" "Shall I go look for him?"

"I think I need to go *now!*" "I've already written him a note."

Her bag was packed and placed by the door. Gloria picked it up and followed her to the car. "I hate to ask this of you, Diane said, but *Hurry!*"

Gloria rushed as much as she dared, but just then Charles drove into the drive way. She stopped only long enought to yell, "Call the Doctor and tell them we are on the way!" Then she sped out and down the road. Diane was moaning loudly and taking deep breaths of air, trying to control the labor pains. "Hold on, Diane. Hold on!" Gloria said as she guided the car over the gravel. "I'm getting you there as fast as I can."

Moments later she whipped the car into the emergency driveway at the hospital where the attendants were waiting with a wheelchair. They quickly helped Diane out of the car and into the chair and disappeared inside with her. Gloria parked the car and hurried inside. She waited anxiously for Charles.

Almost immediately the Doctor came out of the delivery room smiling broadly. "I know you are not the father" he joked, "But you have a bouncing baby girl."

Charles rushed into the waiting room at that moment. "Is Diane alright?" He asked the Doctor.

"Yes, mother and baby are both doing fine. You will be able to see them very shortly."

Charles embraced Gloria saying, "Thank you for being there for her. The baby is a little early. I thought I had time. I'm sorry I wasn't there to take her."

"What are friends for?" Gloria smiled.

The baby was placed in the incabator near the window where everyone could see her and admire the little darling. Gloria thought she had never seen such a pretty newborn before.

The nurse brought Charles into the room to see his wife. They were *so* proud. The Lord had blessed them with a healthy baby girl and everything seemed to be going right in their little world.

On her return trip Gloria would pass by Cox's place so she decided to stop in and tell him about the baby. He had just finished feeding the cows and was coming to the house. He was as excited about the baby as if it was his own grandchild. He couldn't wait to go see her. They decided to make the trip into town together the next day to see her. Right now they would go over to the Wilcox homestead to check on the children.

When they arrived, the three had received a call from Charles and were very excited about the new baby sister.

Three days later, Diane brought the baby home. They had named her Candace Diane. She was a seven pound delight. Kendra was especially happy about the little bundle of joy. She had always wanted a little sister. She wanted to hold her, change her, bathe her and if she hadn't been nursing, she would have been feeding her.

School would be out soon for Spring break, and then she could take care of the baby all day long. She was a big help to Diane.

It was the third week in February. Cox and Gloria were ready to start working on Marlin's house. The clean up work would be first. Cox backed the pickup up to the back door and they began to fill the bed with trash from inside the house. By noon they had it pretty well picked up. Now they would need some boxes for Carol's clothes. They finished filling the pickup bed with trash from the yard, then drove to the landfill. On the return trip, they got some packing boxes from the grocery store. They wanted to let Marlin decide what to do with his mother's clothing. They folded and packed them for storage, just in case he wanted to keep them for awhile.

Cleaning the yard was quite a chore as Bert had carelessly tossed his liquor bottles, beer cans, pop cans, mower parts, and even some tools into the grass. They would need to bring the mower and hedge trimmers tomorrow. The dead grass and weeds covered the entire yard. The little chicken house was knee deep in dung as was the horse shed. Cox couldn't help wondering what had become of the animals.

Since the weather was so cold, they decided to work on the inside of the house for the rest of the day. On the way home, they stopped to see about getting the utilities turned on so they could have lights, heat and water. It would be three days before that happened.

Three days to work on the future "honeymoon suite." They were enjoying working together, so far at least, so Cox wanted to help Gloria with her painting. She had already bought the paint and other necessities, but she needed his help to move the furnature, take down the drapes and pictures, and then patch the nail holed and other imperfections in the walls.

This was all new to Cox. He had never been involved in a painting projet before and was fasinated by Gloria's knowledge of how it should be done. He never resented her instructing him. He was a quick learner and thououghly enjoyed the work. It was pleasing to him to step back and see what a difference they had made. He thought he might enjoy painting as an occupation.

At the end of the three days, they had the house all put back together, pictures, drapes and all. It looked lovely. Now it was time to go back to Marlin's place.

Now that there was hot water, Gloria began cleaning the kitchen. Cox started the mower and worked in the yard. Then he started on the Chicken house. He found liquor bottles hidden in every possible hiding place. He hauled the manure to a place outside the yard for a compost heap, and then went to help Gloria.

The week end came up fast. Cox always looked forward to that. He would have a date with Gloria on Saturday night, Church on Sunday and the counseling session with the pastor. Before he had time to think about it, Monday morning would roll around.

This next week would be the last week in Frbruary. Their marriage date was March 7th. Everything was ready that could be done ahead of time. He and Gloria had purchased matching wedding bands, bought their wedding garments, ordered flowers, etc.

The Church ladies were doing the reception following the ceremony. Rooms were reserved for his siblings and Gloria's children. Everyone in the wedding party was outfitted in the proper attire. Gloria's Grandson would be the ring bearer.

He was very excited about the wedding and went around growling. His mother asked him why he was doing that. In the innocent way of any five year old boy he answered, "If I am going to be a ring bear, I have to practice!"

The next few days whirled by like a top. The big day finally arrived and people came from far and near. The Church house was filled to overflowing with well wishers. Chip, Laura, and Rush came early with their families. They were amazed at how young and handsome Cox looked his *three piece suit, and tie and the little hankie tucked in his breast pocket!* It was a truly joyous occasion.

Everything looked magnificent. The decorations were gorgeous, and the flower girls were beautiful. The musicians began to play "Pomp and Circumstance" as Charles and Cox stood side by side at the alter waiting for the big moment when the bride walked down the aisle on her uncle's arm. Everyone rose and gazed admiringly, at Gloria in her long pink wedding gown, with the lacey veil flowing over her head and shoulders. She carried a boquet of burgandy roses highlighted with delicate baby's breath.

Cox was so overcome with emotion he almost fainted. He took a deep breath and stepped forward to take Gloria's hand. In his wildest imagination, he had not pictured her as lovely as she looked at that moment, and to think, she would soon be *his* wife!

Soon, the ceremony was over and they stood together as man and wife being congratulated by all these good people who loved them. It was almost more than Cox could comprehend. He had lived 28 long painful years without friends or family, and now it seemed to him that *everyone* was his friend. He was extreamly happy!

With rice in their hair they raced to the car, and found it labeled, "just married" in huge letters across the rear window. A string of tin cans and old shoes were tied to the bumper. Suddenly, every horn in the vacinity began blaring. They sped away quickly, followed by a parade of vechicles honking loudly as they raced away to begin their new life together.

EPILOGUE

Cox and Gloria are happily married, Marlin has found that special place, where he feels needed and loved, little Candice Diane is thriving and happy, and the dream of a home for boys is on the horizon.

The end

"Lord, you know the hopes of the helpless. Surely you will hear their cries and comfort them. You will bring justice to the orphans and the oppressed, so mere people can no longer terrify them."Psalms 10:11 -12 (New Living Translation)

Watch for the sequel: "COME HOME, BOY!"